D0502226

# Stormwitch

# Stormwitch

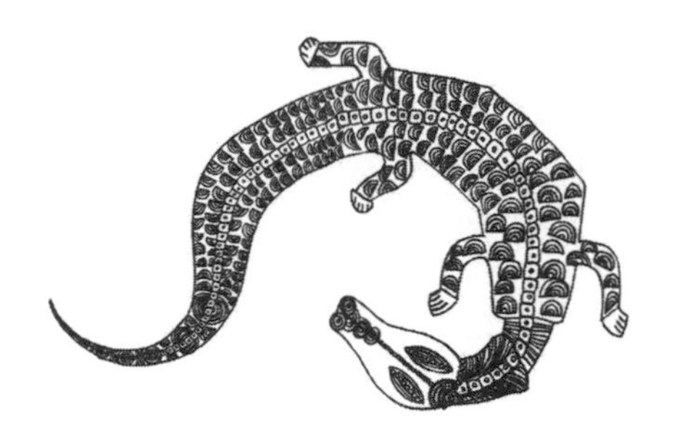

Susan Vaught

BLOOMSBURY

## Acknowledgments

I would like to express my gratitude to Victoria Wells Arms and Jennifer Ward for their patient teaching, shaping, and guidance; to Erin Murphy, my agent, for her skilled marketing and belief in the story; and to my critique partners, Debbie Federici and Sheri Gilbert, for sharp eyes, tireless readings, and equally tireless encouragement. Much appreciation to my grandfather, John Vaught, for instilling in me my love for the Gulf Coast. Thank you to Gisele for your love and patience. Last but not least, thank you to my children, Gynni and JB, for always waiting for the next chapter.

Published by Bloomsbury Publishing, New York and London
Distributed to the trade by Holtzbrinck Publishers

Library of Congress Cataloging-in-Publication Data
Vaught, Susan.
Stormwitch / Susan Vaught.—1st U.S. ed.
p. cm.
Includes historical notes about events and topics mentioned in the story.
Includes bibliographical references (p. ).
Summary: In Pass Christian, Mississippi in 1969, sixteen-year-old Ruba, trained by her Haitian grandmother in both voodoo and Amazonian warrior tactics, uses her skills to fight against racism and the African witch Zashar, now coming ashore in the form of Hurricane Camille.
ISBN-10: 1-58234-952-5 • ISBN-13: 978-1-58234-952-7
[1. Voodooism—Fiction. 1. Hurricane Camille, 1969—Fiction. 3. Racism—Fiction. 4. Civil rights movements—Fiction. 5. Haitian Americans—Fiction. 6. African Americans—Fiction. 7. Hurricanes—Fiction. 8. Pass Christian (Miss.)—History—1969—Fiction.] I. Title: Stormwitch. II. Title.
PZ7.V4673St2005 [Fic]—dc22 2004054681

First U.S. Edition 2005
Printed in the U.S.A. by Quebecor World
1 3 5 7 9 10 8 6 4 2

Bloomsbury Publishing, Children's Books, U.S.A.
175 Fifth Avenue
New York, NY 10010

All papers used by Bloomsbury Publishing are natural, recyclable products made from wood grown in well-managed forests. The manufacturing processes conform to the environmental regulations of the country of origin.

for the real Gisele

*5 August 1969*

*Dearest Ba,*

*Three weeks have passed since I saw your smile, since I had your guidance. It feels like three years. I'm practicing my letters and my writing, do you see? Just like you always wanted me to do. I'm writing in English so I practice the language. Are you proud? You always tried so hard to teach me.*

*It may be cheating, to write instead of speaking out loud. Writing makes it easier to find the words. The words sound too harsh, though. I can't imagine our African foremothers singing of great battles in English. French, maybe. But never English.*

*It's been another long day, and Grandmother Jones seems no happier with me. She called the islands "backward," and when she caught me dancing the way you taught me, she swore I was Satan's tool. I've never known a woman—or a place—so far from Haiti.*

*I thought Mississippi would be like Haiti. Like home. But, Ba. These waters are brown, not blue. The beaches are straight and blank, and the sand feels filthy with hate and anger. This place might as well be a broken shell lost in the waves. Without love. Without magic. Magic means a fast trip to hell here, and Grandmother Jones seems certain I've booked my passage.*

*Why did I have to come here? Why did she have to be my closest relative? Is living in Mississippi my punishment for being too weak to save you from the stormwitch?*

*It's shameful, but last night I actually wished for the stormwitch to send another spirit, and I hoped that spirit would eat Grandmother Jones. But I'd be alone, then.*

*How can I think such things? She's my father's mother. I should respect her. She took me in, and I'm sure she's doing her best. I* must *respect her, even though she's not a warrior like you were. I can't speak back to her even when she makes me so angry I want to use my battle training against her.*

*And if the stormwitch does send another spirit, I must protect Grandmother Jones. She would never trust me that much, though. Even if she did, I don't know if I would be strong enough to fight the witch's magic alone.*

*I dreamed again last night, of there. Of them, of the past. Our ancestors in Africa, the Fon people from Dahomey. Africa crouched like a cat, dark and burning with the fire of a thousand souls. Night spices hung heavy, and clouds raised fists to the moon. I heard Dahomey drums, and they thundered so loud I thought my heart might wing to the stars. Thump and pound, and pound and pound, until they pulled my spirit down and into the celebration.*

*The war women of Dahomey had won a great battle for their king. What you taught me—I remembered it all, and when I danced with the war women, I named Dahomey's kings back to the time before memory. I named my foremothers, too, and the war women said they were great soldiers. Their eyes were bright and happy, Ba. The same brightness I used to see in your eyes when we danced on the beaches in Haiti. Those women were so tall! Just like you. Tall and strong, and they fired their muskets straight, and all their arrows hit their marks.*

*Will I ever be so strong, so skilled, without you to help me learn?*

*The winds are changing here in Mississippi, Ba. The seasons are moving onward, and I'm afraid even though I know you wouldn't approve.*

*What if the stormwitch does send a spirit to find me?*

*What will happen to my new home—my only home and the only people I've got left—if I don't stop her?*

# CHAPTER ONE

## Friday, 8 August 1969: Morning

"Ruba. Ruba! Up, child. You need to get your nights and days straightened out before school starts. You've only got a week or two."

I squeeze the worn leather journal curled in my hands, open my eyes, and stare into those of Grandmother Jones. Her skin lies coffee to my ink, rough to my smooth. My hair hangs black and strong while hers curls thin and white above her wrinkled brow. For a moment, I'm amused by how small she is, shorter than me, like the little people in American fairy stories.

"You awake?" Her gaze seems soft. Almost kind.

Warmth floods my chest. "*Oui, Grand-mère.*"

The soft-kind eyes turn to obsidian. Black glass, shining from bloodshot fields. "I told you, quit that French talk. Nobody in Pass Christian will know what you're saying, and besides, it'll make folks nervous. This isn't Haiti."

"*Oui*—I mean, yes, Grandmother." Warmth gives way

to cold rain inside me. I slide to my feet still squeezing my journal, wishing I could have stayed in my dreams. Wishing my day would hurry by so I can write to Ba again, even about the stormwitch and other dark thoughts. Somehow they scare me less than this woman.

Grandmother Jones hands me a white cloth dress. “Here. I finally got this made so we can put away those loud African robes. All that color draws attention—and not the good kind. Try it on.”

“Yes, ma’am.” I hesitate, then carefully tuck my journal beneath my pillow before accepting the unexpected gift. Part of me feels joy that she made something for me, and part of me feels horror that she took my real clothes. I rub the cotton between my thumb and forefinger, and I can’t help a single hot tear.

Grandmother Jones makes a lemon face and pats my shoulder. “I know I’m not what you’re used to, and this place—it’s new. But you’ve got to get to know it. And me. We’re all you’ve got left now. It’s time you started letting go of what’s lost before it pulls you down. Got to live on that high plane, march ahead, like Dr. King talked about.”

She stands like a shadow over the sun, casting her small but stern presence through my room. I swallow to keep from crying harder. I didn’t need reminding of my troubles so early this day. Her words bring my old life and my new life fresh to my mind, and I can’t stand to see them next to each other.

The house seems suddenly closed and still around me, all clapboard and flaked paint. It smells of flour and fresh grease. Of starch and old chocolate. No sage. No clove. Dull green beans and dull green peppers dry on strings in the kitchen instead of fruit or cowry shells.

*All that color draws attention. . . .*

Ba kept her home true to Dahomey tradition. Simple and colorful, and full of life. We lived as our foremothers in Africa lived, and I always felt like I belonged. I didn't know how much I loved that until I came here.

In Pass Christian, I'm nothing but a tall oddity to be stared at and "brought up all over again," to hear Grandmother Jones talk. She keeps her home clean and pressed, like her white aprons. For her white job. Working for white men and their white wives. Even their white children. Between them and church, her cooking, her cleaning, and her sewing, I feel like she has no time for me. And I feel like she has no idea what I lost, or what I've got left.

I sniff and wipe my nose, and pull the dress she made me over my head. I'm careful to keep my right side covered so she won't see the blue crocodile tattoo covering my lower belly, hip, and thigh. This she would never understand. It would be something else to upset her. The mark of Dahomey's war women comforts me, though, with its fierce teeth and bright colors. My tears dry themselves, and I rub the ivory bracelet on my left wrist. Another mark of my past. All war women—Dahomey's Amazons—wore the bracelet. I think of my dream, of the tall, strong soldiers, and I find it hard to believe they were destroyed. All but one.

"Ah! You're a vision, Ruba." Grandmother Jones offers me a rare smile. Rarer still, a look of approval. "Proper clothes do you wonders. I wish James Howard could see you now!"

I nod and try not to frown. My father never saw me before, so I can't understand why he would care to see me now. He died in Vietnam after he met my mother at Tougaloo College, and she died from fever before I celebrated my first birthday. I never knew her, and I never knew him. Ba was my mother, my father, my sister—and my friend. The first I saw of Grandmother Jones was the day she came to Haiti to claim me.

Why she did that, I will never know, especially since she thinks me so dirty. Stained, like her old rags, because I believe in magic and spirits and many gods. I would have stayed in Haiti, but I had no one left. Grandmother Jones forced me to come with her to *Les États-Unis,* the United States. To Mississippi. To Pass Christian, where whites own the earth and the sand and the waves, and "colored" find no welcome, even on the beach.

I feel like a fool in my white cotton dress, and I think Grandmother Jones knows this. She probably believes it's good for me and thinks it will teach me humility. Just what I need to bring me down a peg.

*We need to bring you down a peg, Ruba.*

She says that often, along with, *This isn't Haiti, and we don't do those things in America.*

What does she really think of me, past the fact I'm a heathen because I haven't been to proper school and I don't believe in her one god? When I look into Grandmother Jones's endless black eyes, I can't tell.

"You were yelling in your sleep again, child," she says, smoothing my dress and picking off a few loose threads. "Something about a 'stomwish.' "

I shiver. "Yes, Grandmother."

"Stomwish. Is that somebody you knew in Haiti?"

According to my beliefs and everything Ba taught me, if I lie to my elder, I'm cursed. But according to Grandmother Jones's beliefs about gods and magic, if I speak the truth, I'm condemned to a fiery hell.

But truth sits better on my stomach, hell or no hell.

"Not stomwish. Stormwitch."

Grandmother Jones's face twists. "I thought we had an understanding about talk like that in my house. Witches and all such nonsense–from hell, going to hell. And all who believe in them, too. But not you, not yet. God gives some grace time for learning. 'Nothing in all the world is more dangerous than sincere ignorance and conscientious stupidity.' Dr. King said that, you know."

"Beg pardon," I say quickly, hoping to cool her anger. "Ba taught me that the women of Dahomey, Africa, the ones who served the king, sometimes made spells—thought they made spells—to control the winds and the waves. They thought it would help the Fon people win wars. People called the women *stormwitches,* and there's a story about a cruel stormwitch named Zashar—sometimes I have bad dreams about her."

Grandmother Jones goes quiet. Her thundercloud look worsens, then passes. "My great-grandmothers probably knew about such, but we're long past that now. You young folks, always studying Africa like it's some sort of heaven." She waves a hand by her cheek, as if swatting gnats. "Maybe when you introduce yourself at church, you should tell some about Haiti and Dahomey. But no talk of witches or conjuring. I won't have juju under this roof, or in God's house."

"Yes, Grandmother." I fidget, thinking about her church.

*Introduce yourself.* That's a step in joining, and I'm not sure if I want to take it. More than that, I dread standing up and facing all those blank eyes and stiff smiles. Most of those people don't know me, and I don't know if

I want to know them. The very thought makes my stomach hurt. My eyes drift to the corner of my journal sticking out from under my pillow

I need to take it and get away from here for a time. I need to write.

Grandmother Jones is talking, and I have to make myself listen as she prattles about the day's plans. "Now, you got grits and bacon on the stove for breakfast–oh, and some biscuits, and I left beans and ham in the icebox for later. And–"

"Yes, ma'am." I can't stand to hear this next part again, so I say it for her. "The number for the Richelieu Apartments is on the wall by the telephone. I'm not supposed to leave our road or the part of beach straight across the highway from us. I'm supposed to say *ma'am* and *sir* to white folks I meet, and keep my eyes on the ground when I say it."

"Good girl. I'll be home around five." Grandmother Jones kisses my cheek and I can't help going stiff like her starched cotton blouse and apron. She keeps telling me this is the way of things in America, and I mustn't speak against it no matter how the television blares of change and revolution. She tells me black people don't have many businesses to hire other black people, that working for white people puts food in our mouths and shoes on our feet.

Me, I could do without the shoes.

I see Grandmother Jones to the door.

One breath of Mississippi brine makes my heart pound in my throat. The breeze smells of salt and wind and storms, with the slightest hint of spice.

Is there a storm coming?

*Is Zashar the old Amazon stormwitch sending a spirit across the sea?*

No. No! Not yet. I can't face her!

"You okay, Ruba?" Grandmother Jones asks as she walks past me and outside, heading for her old yellow and black car.

"Y-yes, Grandmother," I manage.

# CHAPTER TWO

## Friday, 8 August 1969: noon

Before Grandmother Jones has been gone an hour, I've retrieved my journal from beneath my pillow, fastened on my cloth belt and pouch to store shells and herbs, and walked miles from home despite the fact Grandmother Jones wants me to stay in my yard. I can't help it. I feel too trapped, staying on our dead-end street or the little patch of beach Grandmother Jones says is "safe." Still, to please her in some small way, I stick to places where I see black people.

One part of the endless Gulf shore has the whelk I collect to paint. The shelling beach is far down the coast from our street, near a long wharf where shrimp boats come and go. The part nearest the wharf is used mostly by blacks, and I've visited often enough that people have stopped staring at my height and how I sift sand to search for shells.

Ignoring the handful of swimmers, I hunt until I find a few small whelks. Then I settle on a drift of sand to write. Soon, my neighbor Clay and my distant cousin Gisele might come, since their families don't keep them prisoners around their yard like Grandmother Jones would like me to be. Clay and Gisele were born here. They know the rules, and how to take care of themselves. According to Grandmother Jones, I don't know these important things, and I'm having trouble learning.

Clay and Gisele think I'm figuring things out fine. So do I. If they find me, we'll go shelling together before walking home. For now, though, I write, using a small piece of pencil I keep tucked in the book.

*Dear Ba:*

*Grandmother Jones mentioned me introducing myself at her church again. She said I should talk about Haiti. Maybe even about Dahomey. But those people at her church don't really know me, and I don't know them. What if I make them angry? Grandmother Jones gets angry so often when I bring up things from the past, about the way I say things and what I've been taught to believe. Would her church members be any different? I don't know if I want to find out.*

*I'm on the beach again today. The Mississippi Gulf Coast is plain. When I face west along the single ribbon of beach hugging the road—a road that seems to run forever—I see nothing but ocean on my left. No trees, no plants, nothing but sand. On my right, I find the opposite. Almost no sand, all trees and vines and grass with houses, stores, and a few hotels crammed in like mistakes of nature. If I face east, I see the same thing, only with right and left reversed.*

*I know from driving back and forth to the store with Grandmother Jones that all the Mississippi towns run together, from the Alabama line to the Louisiana border. I couldn't tell where one stopped and another began—and I can't now as I squint into the distance. Thickets of pines and palms divide the land on the far side of the road, and they separate houses grander than sugar plantation mansions. Did you ever see the houses white people live in around here, Ba? Did my mother tell you about them when she came home from college?*

*Behind those big houses, less than half a mile from the ocean and still within sight of the waves, shacks like ours hide in little clumps and groups. Our clump, six houses in all, sits at the back side of a dead-end street. The street used to run somewhere, but Grandmother Jones said a hurricane tore it up and the city never built it back. The cars take other roads now, mostly the one highway that separates the beaches from everything else.*

I pause and chew my pencil. In Haiti, cars were few and mansions fewer. Back in Haiti, I walked hours every day, hunting shells and collecting herbs for Ba to make conjure. Few herbs grow wild in Pass Christian, and white people make the evil eye at me if I come too near the places where the plants might be.

Of course, Grandmother Jones would give me an eviler eye if she found my shells and herbs anywhere around her house. The thought makes me laugh, and then it makes me frown. I tuck my pencil in my journal and stare out at Mississippi's brown ocean. It's not always brown. Tides and storms darken it, with sea plants and silt. Sometimes it turns blue, but never clear, and to me it never seems bright.

I want to go home to Haiti so badly my chest aches. The only cure I know is walking, so I get up, slide my journal into one of the two dress pockets, and get moving again. There's no sign of Clay or Gisele, so I head back home.

On the way toward our road, I pass long, clean beaches full of white people sunning themselves, playing radios, throwing beach balls, and riding the waves on floats. They never look in my direction. It's as if I'm invisible because I'm black.

I wouldn't be invisible if I marched out on their sand and caught their ball, would I? And what if I splashed into the ocean beside them? Would they all come running out like I'm a shark?

*Don't think about things like that, child.* Grandmother Jones's voice slips through my mind, unwelcome but forceful. *Laws might keep some people from hurting you, like Dr. King said, but laws won't make them love you.*

In Haiti, all beaches are black beaches. And if Ba had come here to this place years ago when she was still strong and healthy, she would have walked where she chose, when she chose, and dared anyone to stop her. I know in my heart I'll never be the warrior she was, Dahomey Amazon blood or no. I can't bring myself to stroll out on that beach alone.

Grandmother Jones is so different from Ba. She would have me be peaceful all the time, no matter what's done to me. She would have me never give thought to stirring up trouble by invading the white beach. *Live and let live, leave well enough alone*—those are her Christian ways. I don't think I can follow in her footsteps, either. My thoughts and wishes come as they will, and I know one day soon I'll do . . . something outside what she considers peaceful. I just don't know what that something will be.

My stomach twists and starts to burn. I can't be as good a warrior as Ba, and I can't be as peaceful as Grandmother Jones. When real troubles come—like the storms Ba and I used to fight—what will I do then? Scream and run away? Battle and lose? I feel like a failure before I even try.

Long minutes later, I turn onto another "colored" strip of beach full of dark skin and big, welcoming smiles. Black people.

*Colored* people. The word still sounds odd to me. As if

I might be purple or green. *Colored.* Grandmother Jones uses it. Drills me on it. Insists I say colored to refer to my skin when I speak of it out loud. Some people around here say *Negro*. Pronounced Nee-grow, or Nih-grah. Some even use another word. A hard, ugly-sounding word, nothing like the way we mention our color in Haiti. There, *Negro* was said with a roll of the tongue. Neh-gro. Black. Beautiful. The word and our skin.

Nearby, a transistor crackles. When I glance up, I see it's the property of a fat-cheeked boy with skin almost as dark as mine. He holds the radio out as I approach, and I stop to listen to it for a moment.

"Not a cloud on the horizon, folks," the radio announcer says as I hold it to my ear. "Y'all ordered sun, and sun y'all got!"

Music follows, and it has a beat. I kick sand and dip my hips and think of Haiti. The boy giggles, but a thin, harsh voice makes him jump.

"Well, look here. It's the juju girl. Where'd you learn to dance like that, coon?"

I hand the radio back to the fat-cheeked child. He tucks it under his arm and runs, kicking wet sand into the dirty ocean.

When I turn back toward the beach and the road, three white boys are slouching toward me. I've seen them along the road before, at a distance. Two of them stand square against the sky, as big as me—bigger, and built heavy. I see sunburn lacing through their freckles. These two have passed by this beach before, and hooted and jeered at me when I wore my golden print dashiki—Ba's beautiful African robe.

As for the third, the smaller white boy who called me *juju girl* and *coon,* I've not heard from him before, nor seen him up close. He wears blue shorts frayed to his grubby knees, and his face and his yellow shirt have purple streaks from a grape soda he's drinking. Even his teeth are purple. He looks younger than me, maybe by several years. I figure him for twelve, or maybe thirteen, but he acts like I should think he's older.

"Answer me." The boy's ice-blue eyes blink beneath hair so blond it shines. "Look at them beads. That bracelet. You straight from A-freek-ah?"

Around me, colored people scatter like ants. I'm suddenly alone in a crowd as people open a wider and wider circle. I clench my fists. This little boy, he spits cruel words like poison, like they give him some special power.

If I were Ba, I would draw my *couteau*—my knife—and cut him some manners. If I were Ba, I would hex his fortune ruined—and maybe still I would cut him. If I were with Ba in Haiti, I might slap him. But I'm alone, in Pass Christian, Mississippi, and this piece of nothing thinks he's my master.

With the training I've had from Ba in fighting, I could hurt him. I probably could kill him, and I might not be sorry. But Grandmother Jones would never forgive it. I'd lose my home again. I'd be arrested and even more lost, so I don't. Instead, I grind my teeth, lower my eyes, and force myself to answer in the way I've been taught.

"I'm from the West Indies, sir."

The boy snickers. "Why'd you come here? Got all the darkies we need in Mississippi."

His friends laugh as I shrug and study my toes. My muscles tense and my fingers flex, itching to teach these three what it means to disrespect a descendant of Dahomey's war women.

"What's that in your dress pocket? A book?" The boy points a purple-stained finger at my journal, and I put my hand over it before I can stop myself.

"Why don't you read it to us? You can read, can't you?"

He reaches toward my journal, and I look up, glaring straight into his eyes.

Daring him to touch it.

The blond boy's sneer doesn't falter, but he puts his hand down. His cheeks turn pink beneath the purple stains of his drink, and his smile turns frozen.

"She's gonna mess with you, Ray-boy," one of his friends says.

The boy's temper is instant. "Shut up, Dave Allen." To

me he says, "Give me that book."

I don't answer, but I keep my hand where it is.

Ray-boy sticks out his hand again. "Give it here before I hurt you, girl."

Slowly, carefully, I shake my head *no*.

As much whining as growling, he shouts, "Give me that stupid book!"

I'm ready to fight to keep my journal, but a man interrupts us.

"Ray-boy!" he calls from the sidewalk.

For a moment, I hope the man will force the boy to apologize, or at least shame him for trying to steal my journal. As he strolls up behind these large-eared monsters, I give up that hope. His face swells red beneath scraggly stubble, and his eyes are flat and mean. The stench of sour beer and sweat surrounds him as he claps his hand on purple-tooth's shoulder. "This gal givin' you some lip, son?"

The boy hesitates, seems to weigh telling on me against the fact that he still doesn't have the book he demanded.

"Naw, Daddy," he says. "We's just funnin' her."

The man grunts. He eyes me for a second, long enough to make my heart beat faster with worrying about what he'll do. Then he grunts again.

"It's time for the meeting. You can have your fun later."

And with that, they leave me standing, my hands still in fists. I shake from my chin to my toes, grateful for the precious weight of my journal in my pocket.

*You will die,* I think at the man's back as he walks away, *once for each time you insult me.*

But I regret the death-wishing before the thought finishes. I've never been comfortable wishing death on anyone even though my foremothers made many such curses. If an Amazon of Dahomey fell in battle and couldn't be retrieved by her fellow soldiers, she would lie bleeding and screaming and cursing, and kill any enemy who tried to give her aid. If she had no weapon, she'd use her brine-hardened fingernails and filed teeth to tear out throats and gouge eyes.

Such fierceness was admired. Ba would have been that fierce. She wanted me to fight like that, too. I tried, but in Haiti, I was too happy to get that angry. Now, I understand better.

I start to walk after the man and the boys, but a small woman with hair as white as Grandmother Jones's grabs my elbow. "Be still. Don't you say a word, girl. That's Leroy Frye. He's Grand Wizard in these parts."

"Grand Wizard?" The phrase sounds ridiculous to me. "What kind of wizard is he?"

"Sheets, girl! The Knights! Ain't you ever heard of the Ku Klux Klan?"

# CHAPTER THREE

## Friday, 8 August 1969: Afternoon

"I keep telling you the beaches are open now, Ruba." Clay Potts, my neighbor, shakes his head not five minutes after they meet me. We're still close to the spot where I saw the Grand Wizard of the Ku Klux Klan, but we're moving away quickly as Clay lectures. He's seventeen, a year older than me, and he thinks he knows everything. "You don't have to stay on that nasty piece of sand just because it used to be the colored section."

"Nasty sand," Gisele agrees. My cousin is only seven, but she has metal in her eyes. She's been without a mother since she was a baby, according to the stories I've heard. Her mother was killed in the Civil Rights marches. But Gisele has her mother's eyes, everyone says. The metal sparks when her temper flares.

Gisele walks beside me, holding my arm with her strong little fingers. The three of us have walked together like this almost every day, since I first came to Pass Christian. Besides chores and swimming, there is nothing else to do.

"Grandmother Jones wants me to keep to the beach in front of our house," I remind Clay. "She doesn't want trouble at work."

"Daddy says trouble finds you when it wants you," Gisele mutters. "Ain't no sense dodging it."

"Mm-hmm," Clay agrees as we pass the Richelieu Apartments. "Can't spend your life stepping aside to let trouble pass."

Somewhere on the third floor of that building behind him, my grandmother cleans and cleans and hopes trouble will pass. I don't agree with that choice. Ba wouldn't have either. Amazons led attacks in battles. They didn't wait for the war to come to them. I slip my free hand in my pocket and touch the spine of my journal. I've written much of what Ba taught me about Dahomey and the war women between the scarred flaps—part to honor her, and part so I won't forget.

Clay flicks a stone toward the sand. "Woman as smart as Mrs. Jones, tending Whitey's house, minding Whitey's business. Damn shame. She ought to own the Richelieu, hard as she works."

"I tell her that," I say. "But she gets ill with me."

"She probably doesn't mean any harm when she gets mad, you know." Clay grins as he gazes off in the distance, like he's remembering something funny, or maybe he knows something I don't. "It's just her way. Is she still on you to speak up in church?"

The muscles in my neck go tight. "She mentioned it this morning. I don't think she'll give up."

"Probably not. She's like Mama." Clay keeps on grinning in his know-it-all way. "Wants you to mind and act right, won't take any lip, and church, church, church. Hard to believe they were ever loud enough and wild-minded enough to march for Civil Rights."

An image of Grandmother Jones, decked in her Sunday-flower finest and walking for freedom, flickers across my mind.

I reject it.

Civil rights—the more I learn of that struggle, the more I respect any man, woman, or child who took part. But Grandmother Jones? If I had not seen a newspaper photo from Clay's scrapbook, a picture of her stony face in a crowd back in 1963, I wouldn't have believed she had lifted finger or foot for the Movement.

Clay's mother, Miss Hattie—now, she has a face like an Amazon, hard and strong and unforgiving. She has an Amazon mouth, too. That woman's tongue could shell a crab and have words left over. I could imagine her marching. I could see her leading the way and daring anyone to stop her. But Grandmother Jones . . . no.

Does her blood really run in my veins?

Clay takes us toward Blankenship's Drugs. "Black Power's where it's at," he says. "That's what's happening now. We should go right in that drugstore and eat at the counter. What good are the new laws if we don't exercise our rights?"

Gisele and I don't answer. We know better.

"'We must make our own world, man.'" Clay's making-a-stand voice sounds loud in the hot, damp air. "That's what Amiri Baraka says."

I know from previous conversations that Amiri Baraka is a poet who once was called LeRoi Jones. Clay thinks the African name the poet chose is more beautiful than the name his family gave him. After Leroy Frye on the beach, I don't like the sound of LeRoi. And I *hate* Jones. So I agree. Amiri Baraka is a fine name.

"Baraka," I say, letting the syllables sing in my mouth. Perhaps I will change my own name.

"'And now, each night I count the stars,'" Gisele murmurs. Perfect. Doesn't sound like a little girl. Barely even a southern accent, as if speaking a dream. "'And each night I get the same number. And when they will not come to be counted, I count the holes they leave.'"

We stop and stare at her.

"That's part of Baraka's 'Preface to a Twenty Volume Suicide Note,'" Clay says. "How do you know that?"

Gisele shrugs. "Daddy likes it. He says it to me every

night, 'cause of the last part about a little girl talking to her hands. I like the part about stars and holes. You believe stars leave holes if they don't come out, Ruba?"

I think about Ba and I nod. A hole where a star should be.

Clay looks mad because Gisele knows something he doesn't know about his favorite poet. "One day, the Black Panthers'll come down here and leave some holes. And we *are* going to sit at Blankenship's main counter, the one that used to be 'white-only.'"

"Daddy says they're violent," Gisele mutters. "The Panthers."

"So?" Clay shrugs. "Sometimes that's what it takes. Besides, I don't think they're violent. Just . . . loud. And proud. They don't lie down when somebody tries to step on them. What's wrong with that?"

"Grandmother Jones doesn't like the Panthers," I say.

Clay laughs. "That's because she's old school. She worked with the Delta Ministry and all."

I fish through my memory for what I know about the Ministry and find nothing. I sigh. Who can remember all the American political groups? Grandmother Jones has tried to teach me all the important ones. Clay goes over them and over them, like they're spells or holy words. It reminds me of those books in the Bible that talk about nothing but who begat whom. After a while, when

Grandmother Jones reads those parts out loud, she sounds like a bee buzzing on about nothing.

CORE sticks in my mind, because it's a real word. The Congress of Racial Equality. *Core* means the center of a fruit to me, the truest, strongest part that stays when everything else gets eaten—and the part that usually holds the seeds. So I think of CORE as the group that stayed in Mississippi when everything else got eaten. SNCC is the only other one I remember most of the time—the Student Nonviolent Coordinating Committee. Clay's stories about Freedom Summer stick that student committee in my thoughts, especially how they walked right out into the fields to talk to workers, and how a lot of them got bombed and beaten up. He describes Freedom Summer in so much detail it's hard for me to believe it happened five years ago. To listen to Clay, Freedom Summer was yesterday.

The Black Panthers are much easier to think about, because they're happening now and Grandmother Jones doesn't much like the way they do things. *Panther* makes me think of the leopard, Dahomey's royal symbol. War women in Dahomey were also called Wives of the Leopard—the king. It helps me when I'm angry or sad to see myself like that, as fierce enough to be a Wife of the Leopard.

In Haiti, there weren't any groups like the Black

Panthers. We had only nationals and rebels. In the Africa I learned about, there were two groups as well—Dahomey's Fon and their enemies. Black people fighting black people, so often and so hard they couldn't even think about fighting white people if they needed to.

When I first came to Mississippi, I thought it was different here, that black people fought white people instead of each other. Now I know that's not true. Grandmother Jones and black people who think like her fight with black people who think like Clay.

*Like me?*

Clay is still talking. Clay is always talking. He says the time is now for black people in America, and he tries to get me to say *black* instead of *colored*. I do my best, but Grandmother Jones's drills are hard to overcome. Even Crazy Sardine, Gisele's daddy, who lives with her in the house beside us with his two-foot Afro and giant platform shoes, still says *colored* instead of *black* half the time.

And he reads poem-songs to his little girl at night. That I did not expect, though I've gotten the feeling that Sardine and Gisele may know more than they show—about everything and everyone. Like Ba. Like other people who know about history and magic.

My mind turns back to what I heard on the beach about Ray-boy Frye and his father. "What do you know about wizards in the Ku Klux Klan, Clay?"

Clay stops dead in the road. I see tar bubbles snap near his worn white sneakers. "You know I hate talking about the Klan. Gisele's not old enough—"

"Shut up," Gisele says angrily, eyes sparking. "I'm plenty old enough to hear anything *you* got to say, Clay Potts."

He shrugs. No intention of answering me, I can tell, but I keep talking. "This boy at the beach today, and his father, a Ray-boy and Leroy Frye—"

"Man, Ruba." Clay lifts his shoe and pops more tar bubbles. Snap. Snap. "They're the worst trash in town."

"But what about these wizards?" I ask. "Grandmother Jones warned me about the Klan, and you told me a lot about them, but you never mentioned wizards. Are they powerful?"

"It's not what you think." Snap. Snap!

Gisele squeezes my arm hard because Clay's angry. The fast kind of mad, like when your heat rises and your teeth clamp shut and you make fists without even meaning to.

I know better than to say anything to somebody who looks like that, so I wait.

"They don't have any real wizards," he says. "They just call themselves knights and dragons and other dumb stuff, to sound all righteous and scary. Bunch of crackers in sheets, burning crosses and acting big. Easy to string up a man when you got him outnumbered ten to one."

Gisele shudders but keeps her fire eyes on Clay's face.

My throat tightens and I rub it with my fingers.

*String up a man,* he said. Like beans and peppers. Like fruit or shells. I see a horrid mind-picture of people hoisted by the neck and left to dry like spice or produce. Thrown to the gulls like scraps.

These Klux men don't have any real magicians like I feared when I heard the word *wizard,* not if they kill just to be killing. "So . . . the Klan doesn't conjure?"

"Don't be stupid." Clay's irritation hisses through his words. "Of course they don't conjure. No one conjures. That's superstition and nonsense. Slave stuff. It's 1969! Did you live under a rock in Haiti?"

"No. We lived on the beach!" My brain squirms with confusion. That man, that boy—they seemed so powerful. Acted so powerful, for those few minutes on the beach. "Why did that boy call me juju? How does he even know about juju?"

"What do you know about it?" Gisele asks fast, as if she's been waiting to do it since she met me. "Daddy told me Haiti's lots like Africa, even though it ain't far from here. Daddy says lots of people in Haiti still do African spells. You do African spells, Ruba?"

I don't want to answer, so I pretend to ignore her.

Clay acts like she didn't speak. "Ray-boy was running

his mouth, that's all. Juju's an insult, like all the other cracker things they say." His eyes go distant, and I can tell he wants away from this conversation. "Where's your gold dashiki, anyways? Looks better than that dress."

"Grandmother Jones packed all of my African clothes in a trunk."

"I like that red robe you wore last week," Gisele says. "It's pretty. And the blue and pink one."

"They're all beautiful, Sister," Clay agrees. "You should wear them proud." He struts with one finger pointed toward his knee. "What do you want?"

"Black Power," Gisele and I say together, mostly to shut him up.

I lift the collar of my plain white frock and feel like a dozen fools. "Grandmother Jones doesn't want me in my African colors. She says this dress suits my station."

Clay rolls his eyes. "We have to get her into this century, Ruba."

This time, I don't answer. I'm thinking about Ba again, and how she said even centuries can't fix some problems—like Zashar the stormwitch, like the witch's grudge against my family and all white people. Zashar hated the Amazons who supported the rightful king instead of the imposter she chose to help steal Dahomey's throne. She hated the white slavers and slave owners for what they did to Dahomey. It doesn't matter to her that it's history now, not even a little. There's no reasoning with her. When she comes, we just have to fight her—every time, until she's gone or we're gone.

I figure centuries can't fix the Klan, either, with its fake wizards and knights and dragons. Or Grandmother Jones, with her endless quotes and closed-up mind. She believes what she believes, no changing it, just like that vengeful witch.

The ocean suddenly pulls my attention and I look toward the horizon. It's so clear. Not even a streak of clouds.

The stormwitch can't be up to her old tricks. She just can't be.

But if she is . . . if I have to chant a storm she meddles with, I'll have to do it alone. Would these people here, my "family" now—could they possibly let me face what I'll have to face and not interfere? Could they help me if I needed help?

I hold Gisele's hand tighter and blink at Clay's swinging shoulders. "If we got into trouble, would you trust me, Brother?"

"That's a stupid question," he says.

"But would you?"

Clay stops jiving and shrugs. "I guess. Why?"

"No reason," I say, and hope I'm telling the truth.

# CHAPTER FOUR

## Friday, 8 August 1969: night

"Heard about you kids at Blankenship's today." Grandmother Jones offers me a bowl of butterbeans.

"Yes, ma'am." I battle dread and serve myself a spoonful of green lumps, trying everything on the table like I'm supposed to. In these small things, I try hard to make this grandmother happy. "Clay took us for a malt."

"Sat at the front counter, Officer Bolin said."

"Yes, ma'am."

Grandmother Jones has on her rock face, the one with no smile or frown. Not one single twitch or line to hint at what she's feeling, or where she might be headed. She reminds me of Pastor Bickman, making one of his long pauses during a sermon. He says he does that to make us think.

I think he does it because he forgets his next line, but I've never challenged him. Small things to make Grandmother Jones happy.

*Like introducing myself at church. Would it hurt me to do*

*such a little thing?*

Even as I think that, my stomach clenches. I feel like if I take such a step, everything I've ever known might just . . . dissolve.

Grandmother Jones looks anything but happy as she says, "Hearing from the police makes me nervous, Ruba. You know that officer, he wasn't being nice, telling me what you've been up to. He was warning me because you're new around here. And different."

"Yes, ma'am. But the front counter at Blankenship's isn't white-only now. Clay says it's legal and we should—"

"It's legal, child. In Mississippi, lots of things are legal. That doesn't mean they're accepted. Or smart. Blankenship's, the white-only beach, some of the schools—white folks still have spots they'll rise up about."

"Why should we deny ourselves so white folks won't rise up?" My voice comes out louder and higher than I intend. The hot feeling in my chest surprises me. "Why shouldn't we push for our rights, like Clay says?"

Grandmother Jones lays her fork on her plate. She rubs her eyes as if she has not slept in days. "There's pushing, Ruba, and then there's shoving. People fight back when you push, but they fight crazy when you shove. Like Dr. King said, we can't allow our protests to degenerate into physical violence."

The heat in my chest rises to my throat, my face. If she had any idea what Ba was, what I am—how could I ever learn to just push when I've been trained to shove?

It's all I can do not to yell when I speak. "Should we pretend laws don't exist just so we don't make white folks angry? Just so they don't get violent?"

"Child, you've been here three weeks." Grandmother Jones stands. Abandons her plate, and me, and bothers with pots on the stove. "I've been living in this place my whole life. You're as bad as the Student Nonviolent kids, down from the North a few years back."

I jump to my feet, feeling like my blood is on fire. "Clay told me the Student Nonviolent Coordinating Committee brought volunteers. Risked their lives, got beat up and killed—and still kept fighting! Got the people registered. Got them to vote."

Grandmother Jones sighs, and I see her shoulders sag. "It's more complicated than that. Freedom Summer—the volunteers—don't go making it some sweet dream. There were good things that came of it. And bad."

"What bad things can come of good change?" I demand.

"People dying." Grandmother Jones turns. She wields the spoon from the butterbean pan like a knife, pointing it. Sauce drips on the floor. Her rock face shatters into dark, shifting sand. Rearranging in ways I don't like.

"You listen to me, and listen good, Ruba Jones. Freedom isn't worth much if you're too dead to enjoy it. Like poor Gisele's mother. I swear . . . Now sit your butt down and don't open your mouth cross to me again, you hear?"

I sit.

But I think I wouldn't mind dying for what I believe.

Grandmother Jones lowers her spoon. "Lots of us down here, we didn't want Freedom Summer—not because we didn't want the change, no ma'am. Because we didn't want the deaths, and we didn't want rich Northern white folks taking over our movement and our choices, pushing local folks like Fannie Lou Hamer and Lawrence Guyot aside. We hadn't registered many voters, but our leaders were growing, and we were starting to change. Our way, in our own time."

Slow, I think. Slow, slow change. Anything Grandmother Jones would approve of, it would have to be slow and safe.

"But SNCC came," she says, pronouncing it *snick*. "And the changes came faster, and all that's good. Won't take anything away from any of those folks risking what they did. They're all heroes, if you ask me. Every one of them. But it didn't end there. Our problems didn't go back North with them. This isn't a bedtime story, and we're not living happy ever after."

I think hard about how I know that. How this woman must think I'm stupid.

"Lots of SNCC's volunteers stayed after Freedom Summer. And they did good things—but the Movement's different down here now. Mrs. Hamer said it a few years ago. The Mississippi Movement's gotten colder. Bigger. Less love and acceptance. And kids like Clay and you, y'all are impatient and angry. Demanding new answers to old questions—and fast answers. I just don't know if y'all will move us forward or drive us back in the long run. Or do both at the same time, like Freedom Summer did."

I don't answer, because I don't know what to say. I've lived here only three weeks, and every day I feel unfairness and injustice. It settles on me like ropes, and it burns. I'm burned with Grandmother Jones. With older people. With white folks and the white world. I want to go back to Haiti. To a place with ten thousand black faces. Ten million. A place that might make some sense.

My fingers curl, and I stare at my plate. I would die. Yes, I would die rather than live like a less-than forever.

Grandmother Jones sits. As if reading my mind, she makes her face a stone again. Or wood. Like carved mahogany, weathered and scarred. "Y'all are so ready to die. But if you're patient, if you push instead of shove, maybe you won't have to die so fast, and change can still happen. Sometimes a little push is plenty enough to get things moving."

I force myself to nod, but I find my eyes leaving Grandmother Jones. Studying the floor. The wall. Anything. She doesn't understand what I feel.

"Eat your dinner, child," she says. "Please."

I jam a spoon into my butterbeans and dump the lumps into my mouth. Chew the hateful things. Like wet paper. No taste at all.

Grandmother Jones studies the ceiling. "Time was, sitting at a white-only counter would get us arrested. That, or parking too close to a fire hydrant halfway around the block. Or reckless driving when you haven't even moved your car. Every day, you had to watch. Every step, looking over your shoulder. Behind you. Beside you. Worrying, and wondering, and waiting. I'm not sure how much better it is now."

Her voice sounds far away. Like she is not even talking to me. "Mississippi's hard. Mississippi's the worst of the worst, like they said. And this fight, it's far from over, Ruba. I hope you realize you've landed in the middle of a battle bound to last your whole life. Don't spend all your rage these first weeks. You'll need it later."

I still say nothing, but something inside me stiffens. What does this woman know of fighting? This battle or any other? Her job, her life—she's busy hiding from trouble. That much seems as clear as the stained-glass dove in her precious church's biggest window.

"Guess all of life's a fight." Grandmother Jones shakes her head. "One time I got my jaw busted, over at Blankenship's, because I sat to eat my hamburger where I bought it. At least they didn't mob me and smear me with ketchup and mustard like they did Pearlina Lewis and Anne Moody at Woolworth's up in Jackson. That was a scene. Hundreds of people. A riot—one boy almost got killed."

My butterbeans stick in my throat, and I force them down with a sip of sweet tea. Curiosity shoves my anger aside faster than I can take another breath. "Did you—at Blankenship's—when you went in, did you . . ."

I try, but I can't ask the question. Doubt I can believe the answer.

"Go to Blankenship's and do it on purpose?" Grandmother Jones's rock face doesn't crack. Not a single chip. "My boy and your mother, they would have done it if they'd been here. But they weren't, so somebody had to. Lord, but those girls in Jackson, they were just kids. Not much older than you."

She goes right on eating, as if she has not shattered my perceptions of her like a thousand stained glass doves flung against rocks. And she shows no emotion.

Grandmother Jones talks about courage, about facing hate, all with less feeling than when she orders me to look at my feet and be polite around white people.

*Like Ba spoke of the war women and their killing. Matter of fact. As if it's something anyone would do, given the same choices.*

A numbness creeps into my mind. Up until now, I've seen mostly differences between my two grandmothers. Now, a sameness I didn't expect.

And yet, my temper won't be quiet. How could Grandmother Jones show her courage and expect me to put mine away? Why would she want me to keep my eyes on the ground?

I can't find the nerve to ask. That might earn a day's cold silence. With this strange woman, who can tell?

"Did you and Ruba Cleo—your Ba—actually trace the family back to Africa?" she asks before I recover my balance from her first set of surprises. "I know lots of Haitians come from there because of slaving. But have you really been able to reach all the way back to Dahomey?"

The potatoes on my fork feel heavy. I open my mouth. Close it. What do I say?

"We have the song," I finally manage.

"What song?"

"W-with a drum, we sing our mother's names, back to

the guards of Dahomey's first king. Past that, we can't know, since mothers weren't named."

Grandmother Jones stirs gravy in a dish, slow circles, as if she might divine truth from grease and browned flour. "Why didn't women know their mothers back then?"

"Dahomey women did," I explain. "But Amazons weren't regular women. They were soldiers. They were taken from their parents, raised and trained behind palace walls, and they gave up any family ties except loyalty to each other and the king. He was like a god to them. That's why they fought so well, so wild—"

My voice dies in my throat as I see Grandmother Jones's puckered lips. Her furrowed brow. Dread settles on my heart.

"Thou shalt have no other gods before Me," she quotes from her Bible. "Those women shouldn't have seen a king as a god."

I don't answer, and slowly lower my gaze back to my plate.

Grandmother Jones closes the conversation with a cough, and we finish our meal in silence.

Later, in my bedroom, she finds my cloth bag where I stupidly left it out on the bed after my walk today. How could I have been so forgetful?

I wring my hands even as she snatches it up, wrapping

the strings around her knotted fingers. "What's in this?" she asks, swinging it back and forth. "As if I don't know."

She's so short I could just reach down and snatch the bag from her old hands. It would be easy, like taking a bone from a little dog.

But I don't.

"Just herbs," I mutter. "I got them on my walk, so I could—"

"I know what you got them for. I'm not stupid." She opens the bag and pours the herbs and my other secrets into her apron pocket. "Matches and candles, too. Mm-mm. You took these from the church, didn't you?"

Her eyes burn like a thousand lighted candles. "Not in my house, girl. Not now, not ever."

With that, she thrusts the empty bag back at me. "I don't want to take away things your grandmother Ruba Cleo gave you, but if you put anything else in this bag that doesn't belong in my house, I'll be keeping it from then on."

I stare at the bag in my shaking hands. I can't look at her. My muscles feel like sticks jammed under my skin, hard, brittle, ready to snap and just beat on something—probably her—until they break. Or she breaks.

"God forgive this child." She talks in her quiet prayer voice, then puts her cold hand on my cheek. "She doesn't know right from wrong yet. She needs to make herself known to the church, to you, to save her soul from the pit."

"There's a storm coming," I say in a tone that feels part mine, part Ba's. "I sense it. There's something evil inside all that wind. I have to gather what I need to fight it, and you'll have to trust me, or we'll all die."

Grandmother Jones swells, like she's puffing for a rage, but instead she sighs. Her hand stays on my cheek, but the pat becomes a pinch that feels barely controlled. "Don't imagine trouble, Ruba. You got enough that's real right here. God will help us with whatever comes. Witchcraft is the devil's work."

She lets me go. My cheek smarts where she pinched me. I strangle the cloth bag with my fingers.

She leaves, finally.

I'm alone again, finally.

My only comfort is a quick glance at the loose floorboard Grandmother Jones seems not to notice.

At least she didn't find all of my special things, my weapons, hidden under that board. I might have what I need to fight the storm, or most of it—but it won't matter. She'll never trust me.

It takes little time to get into bed, but I can't sleep. Minutes pass, then more and more. Finally, I hug my pillow and cry as dinner churns in my belly. Visions of Ba haunt me. I see her younger and stronger, helping me nock my first arrow, lovingly stroking my shoulder as I fight the string.

*You aren't fast, and that's no shame, girl. The fastest shoot the muskets. Those of us who run slower, we make archers. You and I, we'll work on your arms until they're strong enough to fire as many arrows as it takes. . . .*

I see Ba a year later, looking sicker but smiling at me, stirring fish stew over a fire on the beach. I see her singing to the wind that spring, magic in her voice, bringing rain for our flowers and palms.

I see Ba, eyes bright as we chant to turn that last storm together.

Her teeth stand out, two rows of ivory against her full, soft lips. She blows me a kiss, just like she always does before we chant for the weather. I'm worried because she seems frail from being sick so often, and Ba has never been frail. She tells me she's old now, nearing her end, but I don't want to hear that.

I want to think of her as I see her now, ready to fight the storm. She still has enough magic to chant. Her words won't be frail at all, I know.

"Il n'est pas *Zashar," she whispers as the wind twists toward us. "Next time, it might be her, and we could end this forever. We're the last, child. And the last will have to do what all the rest couldn't. Get rid of that witch once and for all, so storms can be storms, and nothing more."*

Listening with only half an ear, nervous, I study the wind. Ba always talks about being the last, and about one day fighting Zashar. But this isn't the stormwitch. We both know that, because the weather doesn't feel strong enough. The sky doesn't feel dark enough. When Zashar finally comes, she'll come at night, with darkness and screaming wind fit to kill anything in the storm's path.

Still uncertain of what magic we'll have to fight, Ba and I begin the song.

I sing my mother's name. Circe. And then Ruba Cleo—Ba. When it's her turn, Ba sings of Antoinette and Arielle, and back we go, two at a time, to Tata, the first Dahomey Amazon to come to Haiti and survive.

Ba holds Agaja's necklace, in case we need the strength of his spirit.

The wind picks up.

We keep singing, calling on our African foremothers, asking them to protect us and send the hurricane back to sea because it's unnaturally strong, because there's witch work in it. We know the wind carries an Amazon spirit, confused and under the control of Zashar, the stormwitch.

Zashar has been dead a long time, but she refuses to rest in peace. Her hate keeps her forceful, even in the place where the dead stay. She preys on other Amazon spirits, chases them out of the quiet of death, and sends them to do her vengeance on my family, and on white people, too. It's up to Ba and me to break through the battle fever driving those confused spirits, and to show them the truth. To show them who the real enemy is—Zashar and all her hate.

Ba's fingers, oiled for battle, slip against my palm as I try to hold them. In her other hand, she clutches the necklace.

The winds pull and tug. I try to hold my base. Sand swirls, hiding my grandmother. I see nothing but rain and darkness. My eyes water. I forget my words, forget the names I should speak. The wind shrieks, sensing my weakness.

And still, above it all, Ba sings, setting her strength against the storm. She sings of Dahomey's great king Agaja, whose spirit we still serve and carry. She rattles the necklace and tells of how Agaja closed the slave ports and tried to set Dahomey free from wars with other nations.

She tells the storm how Agaja named his fourth son to succeed him, how Agaja believed his fourth son would carry on his traditions. But that wicked son was interested in his own wealth and power. He had his witch Zashar do away with his older brothers. One, a son who truly believed in the ways of his father, was sewn up in a bag with his Amazon guard Tata and thrown into the sea.

Ba tells the spirit in the storm how Tata and the loyal son were supposed to die, but Tata survived. Picked up by Dutch slave traders, Tata came to Haiti, where she guarded the spirit and beliefs of King Agaja. Ba tells the storm how we are Tata's descendants, the last of the living Amazons.

*Wake,* she commands the poor ghost in the wind. *See the truth.*

Zashar wants to kill us because Agaja was right about closing the ports, and his wicked son's decision to trade slaves with the whites destroyed Dahomey in the end. Zashar wants to kill us because we don't believe attacking all white people is the way to fight back against that pain and destruction.

Mostly, though, Zashar wants to kill us because she was an Amazon, and Amazons fight to the death and beyond to protect their king. Tata and our line supported the wrong brother. We were a threat to her king then, and we're a threat to the power of his memory now.

*We speak against the betrayer.*

Ba's voice sounds as loud as the wind, and I shiver from fear and pride.

*We speak against Zashar and the useless hate she spreads. We speak against killing for the sake of killing, and death without purpose.*

Finally, Ba reminds the spirit that she died long ago,

with the rest of the brave war women in those last battles with the French.

The winds sputter and go quiet. We're in the eye.

Ba lowers the necklace and releases my hand, and I grab my bow with trembling fingers. The arrow, tipped with a mix of herbs, spice, and spells to send the spirit back to the land of the dead, shakes as I take aim. I'm ready to shoot if I must. I've been trained. Ba has drilled me like the Amazons of old, as I will drill my daughters and my daughters will drill theirs. Through us, King Agaja's triumphs and the glory of the war women will live forever.

Clouds part.

A woman stands before us, tall like a goddess, eyes dripping lightning like tears.

I know without question which Amazon this spirit is, from the strength of the wind, the brand on her bare chest, and the courage in her wizened face.

She seems as old as mountains. As timeless as dirt and air.

Ba keeps singing to her.

This spirit, Agontime, doesn't rage like other spirits in other storms we've chanted to turn. Dahomey-born and sold to slave traders after a palace coup, Agontime bore the pain of twenty-four years of Brazilian slavery before royal deputies found her and took her home to Africa.

Despite her tragedies, she went on to become adviser to another of Dahomey's most powerful rulers, balancing his strength with grace and wisdom. The name she chose speaks for itself.

Agontime means "monkey who came home from the land of the whites, and now stays in a field of pineapples."

Before us, her great spirit wakes to itself, and perhaps dreams of that pineapple field. She hears Ba's song, and seems to realize that she shouldn't be here, in the land of the living.

I watch as she shudders. Twists.

The spirit fights against Zashar's sorcery, the dark magic the stormwitch uses to drive peaceful souls to despair and rage.

Even in spirit form, Agontime's will proves formidable. Unlike every spirit we've met before, this one realizes who she was in life, what she is now—and where she belongs. She realizes what Zashar's magic has done to her.

With a roar, Agontime turns her majestic back on us and faces east, back across the ocean toward Dahomey. Toward her home.

Her movement catches me by surprise.

None of the spirits has ever turned back home without Ba firing her arrows!

And now this time, my first time as the archer, the spirit turns on her own!

I see her movements as if slowed to half of real time.

Should I fire?

The strength in my arms falters, and my arrow flies by accident. It falls into the sea, useless. Agontime strides away, walking the storm back out into the ocean. Hurricane winds circle and follow her like screaming children.

Ba cries out.

We aren't ready for this. We have no protection from the suddenly shifting winds! Ba whirls. Grabs for my hands. I sling my bow over my shoulder. We lock eyes and fingers, and hold tight against the storm's sudden movement. We hold against the growl of the hurricane, against the fury in the waves—and my memory blurs.

I see Ba's tired face as the water fights to tear her from my grip. The sand beneath her feet gives way into thrashing water. For a moment, she drags me with her as she sinks.

In the distance, Agontime roars on in a language I barely understand.

Then Ba's smiling—why is she smiling?

She looks relieved as she lets go with one hand, to toss Agaja's necklace out of the water. It lands safely beside me.

Ba's speaking, but my ears won't hear her. I'm shaking my head. My hands are shaking, too. Our fingers slip apart.

There's an empty beach where Ba should be.

The ocean . . . the sky . . . a sense of Ba's spirit, rising and rising—and then nothing at all until I wake on the sand.

Cold. Crusted like wood too long in the surf. Cut in a hundred places, with a shell necklace, a broken bow, and a few last wet arrows. And I'm alone.

Alone because I didn't hold tight enough or shoot straight enough. I'm not fast, but I also wasn't strong.

I let go of Ba.

My weakness killed her.

Now as it did then, pain crushes my chest. I feel like my heart is torn in half.

Sobbing, I roll over in my bed in Pass Christian, Mississippi. In the home of Grandmother Jones, a Christian woman who speaks of pushing not shoving, and who thinks witches live only in my imagination. My hand slides under my pillow to find my journal.

For a moment, the cover feels like the oiled leather of Ba's fingers in mine, just before she slipped away. The hole in my heart's sky where Ba's star ought to be opens wider and darker than ever.

Through my window I see a single light, broken from

my tears, shining from Crazy Sardine's house next door. And an outline, small and slight. A tiny shadow.

Gisele. And she's staring at me.

I'm sure of it.

*9 August 1969*

*Dearest Ba,*

*I've come to a terrible suspicion. There* is *a storm coming soon. I sense it's a beast of a storm, too, whipping waves from Africa. It doesn't feel natural, but it doesn't feel like it carries an Amazon spirit, either.*

*It feels darker than that.*

*I'm scared to touch the storm with my mind. I know I'm an Amazon, that I shouldn't be scared, but I can't help it. I keep trying to remember the last thing you said to me on the beach in Haiti. I see your lips moving. I know I heard you.*

*What did you say?*

*Leaves are rustling in the trees outside my window. These people on the Mississippi coast know nothing. They scoop sand and build castles that will be swept away by sea foam. Grandmother Jones—she seems more distant than ever. That woman is a greater mystery to me than ancient riddles. More impossible than Egba's rope puzzles. I will never understand her.*

*And she will never trust me enough to let me fight the storm. She'll interfere. Get us all killed, in the name of her almighty god.*

*Clay told me he trusts me, but I don't know. And Gisele,*

*maybe. Crazy Sardine, perhaps he believes. He seems to have a deeper wisdom, despite his strange appearance. Those long shirts and wide sweeping pants—and gold chains, and his shoes! How can a man walk on stilts with no grips? And yet he gives me the oddest smile when I'm near, like he's known me forever, and he's waiting for me to lead him somewhere.*

*Ba, how will I turn the evil in this storm without you?*

*Grandmother Jones found some of my herbs again, after dinner. She threw them away, and she took my matches and candles. Praise the universe she didn't find my war tunic and cap—or my machete, or my mended bow and the three arrows tipped by your very own hands.*

*She prayed for me, or prayed over me. Said she fears me going to hell. Said I need to make myself known to her church, her god.*

*I told her about the storm I sense, and she told me I was imagining things. I wanted to tell her I know the ways of our people before the Slave Coast betrayed us all, but she's told me over and over that I hold too tight to yesterday. If I swore I heard Dahomey's drums in my dreams, she wouldn't believe me. There are things in this life, of this world and the others, that Grandmother Jones has never seen, and she can't understand them.*

*She wants me to put away my past, Ba. She says I live in a civilized world now—as if a country with the likes of Leroy Frye, Ray-boy, and her white bosses at the Richelieu could be more civilized than Haiti.*

*I don't think anyone here knows about the storm yet, Ba. I'm alone, I'm alone, I'm alone.*

*I want you back.*

*If this storm kills me, I'm not sure I'll care.*

# CHAPTER FIVE

## Sunday, 10 August 1969: morning

Clay, Gisele, and I stretch our legs walking on the beaches that used to be white-only. We thought that by coming on Sunday morning, early, before church, we wouldn't meet too many people. We thought it would be good practice, to help us get our courage up to walk again later, when the beach gets more crowded.

We were wrong.

These folks sure seem set on their Sunday morning swim in the waves.

We march anyway, deliberately walking out of our invisible cage—the one my grandmother would have me stay in, eyes down, mumbling *sir* and *ma'am* to people I don't even know. Her talk of pushing without shoving lingers in my mind, but I keep it to the side. My anger toward the situation is already too great. My hand clenches around the journal in my pocket, and the top of my head aches. I think I might yell at the first person who tries to stop me.

As usual, Gisele walks by my side holding my arm at the wrist. She looks straight ahead, eyes flashing, as we stroll up and back, and up again. White mothers grab their children and glare. Some people point and stare. Some smile, nervous-like. Shy and unsure. A few—three, perhaps four—nod, as if to welcome us.

We cast shadows on the Gulf of Mexico as we pass. Sun beats my skin like hot golden hammers, but what strikes me the most are the people who don't react at all. Seem to see nothing. Watch the air as we walk by, expressionless, as if we are haunts or sea-shines. Blank-facers bother me more than the haters and smiler-nodders. Rocks. Like Grandmother Jones, except these rocks are white.

Who are they? What do they feel?

Do they feel?

A radio spits and fuzzles on a woman's towel.

" . . . tropical disturbance, still more than five hundred miles east of the northern Leewards . . ."

The woman sees me listening and snaps off the power. Then she makes a gesture I'm sure her fellow church members would gasp about.

Clay's version of chanting trips through my mind.

*What do you want? Black Power.*

All the wide eyes and gaping mouths make me think the people on this beach can't imagine *black* and *power* joined in the same sentence. Pass Christian reminds me of towns I saw in my father's photos of Vietnam, the few he sent home to my mother. Ba kept them in an album, so I would have them. That album was full of wide eyes and gaping mouths—empty expressions, tense brows, smiles that pointed to nowhere . . . people at war. Only the people in Pass Christian aren't fighting an army. Mississippi's whites are fighting other Mississippians, black ones—and according to Grandmother Jones, and Clay, and all the books I've read, they've already lost the war. Twice now.

Why don't they know that?

"Bitch," whispers Clay, staring at the woman with the radio.

"Mm-hmm," Gisele says. "Big ole behind, too."

"You don't have to call names," I mutter, though I'm not sure why. It just seems wrong. "That woman is who she is, who her mother raised her to be."

"You really sixteen years old?" Clay shakes his head. "You sound like my great-grandmother."

"In Haiti, we had no time to be young. And back in Africa, people had even less time to grow up. Most war women went to training as soon as they could eat for themselves."

"I eat for myself." Gisele swings my hand. "I want to be a Da-Homely war woman."

Clay groans. "What have you been telling her, Ruba? Living on that island cooked your brains like mackerel. Never mind. Don't even want to know. Let's go down to the wharf instead."

"No," I say. "I need to go to the campground, near the covered gardens."

"You going to pick plants again?" he asks, and I hear another groan coming.

I stroke the soft cloth bag hidden in my pocket beneath my journal. "Grandmother Jones cleaned house again last night. She took all my special herbs, all the ones I need to fight the storm."

"There won't be a storm," Clay mutters. "Hurricanes, they usually swing wide of us. Head for Texas. You and that Dahomey storm magic stuff—when are you going to get over it?"

I refuse to answer him.

Gisele speaks for me. "Be quiet, you ole dummy. She ain't getting over it. She's going to teach me. Starting with which plants we need to chase away the evil in the wind."

"Well, go ahead if you have to, but I'm swimming." Clay runs off toward the water. "Meet you by the campground!"

Gisele and I climb the bank and cross the two-lane, moving away from the beach and toward all the houses and green. Wordless, we head into a thick stand of pines and begin our search. Her hands are nimble, and her eyes sharp as I teach her to seek tiny flowers and roots, shifting sand for shells as she goes.

My bag grows heavy, and heavier still. Gisele drops leaves and little frogs into her pockets when she thinks I'm not looking. And a lizard. And one lost hermit crab. I watch as she giggles and crams her hands through moss, under rocks, behind anthills, never minding the bugs. Scaring snakes to death.

Was I like this when Ba taught me? In a big hurry, taking no time to think or be careful?

Surely not.

Minutes pass. Maybe hours. Time moves in strange ways when you gather plants for conjuring. And the light helps. If you stare at it long enough, it filters through to touch what you need.

Gisele sees this. Her eyes widen as she follows soft rays to a patch of white-yellow mushrooms.

Just then, a terrible racket plagues the bushes behind us. We both startle.

Voices slither through scrub pine and palm. "Know I saw them come in here. Y'all go that way."

Ray-boy.

Mumbles and stomps come next—from his square, stupid friends, I assume.

Ba's teaching overtakes me, and I grab Gisele. She holds me tight, and we join bark and branches without a sound.

"Here, Juju," Ray-boy calls like he's coaxing a dog. "Got something for you. C'mere."

He passes us without a clue.

"Hey, Poke. You see them?"

"Naw."

"Dave Allen?"

"Nah, Ray-boy. They ain't over here."

More footsteps, and then a whirlwind of shouts and bellows.

"Hey!"

"Let me go!"

"Over here, y'all!"

"No! Over here!"

I watch without breathing as Ray-boy Frye and his friends haul Clay toward our tree. Clay fights and swings, but his toothpick fists make no match for the two big white boys.

Ray-boy steps up and puts his face almost nose to nose with Clay. Clay stops fighting and stands still.

"Give me a belt, Poke," says Ray-boy. "We'll do him here, right now."

Gisele shudders. I squeeze her so hard she wheezes, but she holds her noise.

"Your daddy said to wait about this one." The one Ray-boy called Poke stands as large as a man, but he sounds like he has the mind of a toddler.

"Yeah," the other boy, the one who must be Dave Allen, says. "He told us to get that juju girl."

"Daddy won't care. The only good darkie's a dead darkie, right?"

Chills fan my neck and I struggle not to cry out.

Ray-boy takes Poke's belt and cinches it around Clay's neck. I hear him choking, and I can't stand it. Gisele offers no protest as I shift her around my hip. Shield her with my body and outstretched arms.

In my war voice, I shout, "Let him go!"

One heartbeat passes. Two heartbeats. Three.

Gisele's fast breathing is the only sound I hear.

Ray-boy makes a gesture and his friends throw Clay on the ground. Ray-boy puts his foot on Clay's back. "Come on out! Welcome to the party."

I do come out, but in my own time, at my own pace. Ray-boy and his friends stand over Clay and snigger, even as I raise my hands and start a chant. They snigger as I call on Circe and call on Ba, and as I call on my grandmother's mother, and hers before that. My voice takes a rhythm of its own, reaching back. Picking up the rhythm of Dahomey's drums.

Ray-boy finally stops laughing. His lips twitch. "What

are you doing?"

The minute he speaks, Clay scrambles out from under his foot, crawling for shelter behind me. The belt Ray-boy tightened around his neck dangles like a leash.

"Hey, Ray-boy," mumbles Poke. "Is she really a juju girl?"

Gisele takes up my rhythm, humming with no words. Her voice makes mine louder. We're like two drums now.

"Sali and Aja," I sing. "Hwanji and Tata."

When I reach Tata's name, more power rises to my call. Leaves on the trees shake from a strong, sudden wind. They blow and rustle. Rustle and blow.

"I don't like this, y'all." Dave Allen steps backward and trips into the fangs of a yucca bush. "Ow!"

I hold up my hands, stirring the wind as I feel it. My feet do the drumming now.

"Help me, Circe. Help me, Ba. Help me, all the war women who fought for their kings. Help me, Africa's woman heart!"

Wind howls over me now. Whips across my skin. Slams into the white boys like a wall of rage.

Poke stumbles backward, then breaks and runs. Dave Allen curses and fights his way out of the shivering yucca. He crawls away, trailing blood from where the yucca's sharp tips stuck him.

Gisele hums without breathing, without breaking the

beat, as the wind comes again.

"Be gone with you, boy," I hiss to Ray-boy as I dance.

"You calling *me* boy?" he says, half tough. Half scared.

I thrust one hand into my pocket, find my bag, and open it with quick fingers. Inside, I feel shells, a few stones, and pieces of pine bark. They will have to do. I pull them out and fling them into the air.

The wind sweeps up the offering, and thunder bursts over my head.

Gisele screams, but not from fear. Her fierce sound welcomes the weather. Seems to dare it to come again—and thunder booms through the woods.

Rain falls on Ray-boy Frye, harder and harder.

He glares at me.

I glare at him and laugh.

He turns and stumbles away.

I close up my bag and laugh and laugh until I run out of breath.

Gisele laughs, too. A high sound. Thrilled and splendid. She whirls circles in the spot where Ray-boy stood.

I turn to Clay, who has pulled the belt off his neck. He flings it into the bushes, then meets my gaze, quivering and rubbing his throat.

"Trust me now?" I ask.

He nods.

"I trust you," Gisele echoes, still not sounding all the

way like a little girl. Sounding a little old, a little strong with voices of time gone before.

"Come on," Clay mutters where I can hardly hear him. "We need to get home before it's time for morning service, or my mother and Mrs. Jones will skin us for sure."

# CHAPTER SIX

## Sunday, 10 August 1969: Late Afternoon

Pass Christian Missionary Baptist Church waits among scrub pines and knotted oaks at the end of a long dirt drive. It welcomes us for the second time this late Sunday afternoon with soft lights and a milling crowd. Morning service seems like it happened a year ago, and all I can remember of it is turning around about a hundred times to make sure Clay was all right.

He was, of course. But he rubbed his throat a lot.

For this evening service, I'm wearing another new cotton dress, this one yellow. Black shoes pinch my feet despite black stockings. The shoes and stockings are new, too. Grandmother Jones brought them home from work Saturday evening. She tried to make me wear a hat and gloves, but I refused those.

Politely.

As we walk toward the main steps, she holds my arm and beams. I feel like a scrawny giant next to her. She beams at her friends, because I've told her I will introduce myself.

*It's a small thing*, I tell myself.

On the lawn around the church, women in hats and dresses wear white gloves and big smiles, laughing with the men. Men in suits and ties look shaved and scrubbed, fresh like little boys. Little boys hold up chins and act big—except when they rip off their coats and chase little girls. Little girls in dyed cotton and braids dodge the boys and tug ribbons that match their socks.

In Haiti, I worshipped with Ba at our chapel on the beach. Our temple was the ocean. The Catholics let us be, praying behind their mortar and stone, but for the bells that pealed each day to announce the time.

In Mississippi, black folks seem to live and breathe through the Baptist church. And Methodist, and Presbyterian. I suppose the Catholics are here, too, but I've not seen them or heard them singing. Only the single bell from this Baptist Church, where I've come some ten times in three weeks—every Sunday and Wednesday, and extra, when the preacher says to come.

"Every time the doors open," Grandmother Jones likes to say.

I admit there is something of comfort in these worn white boards, in the rambling wraparound porch and smooth, brown pews. And when the people sing . . . when the people sing, I forget my starless heart for long minutes at a time. The church breathes and sways. And I breathe and sway, and when I close my eyes, I can almost hear Dahomey's drums. Sense the Creator on my very skin. In my skin. In the rocking of my heart and the pounding joy of voices around me.

For the singing, and for Grandmother Jones, I come.

For Grandmother Jones alone, I plan to speak. Only for a few minutes. And no mention of witches and conjure, as she wants. This may be my only chance before the stormwitch comes, and I don't want to let her down by refusing, or by saying something that embarrasses her.

And yet I don't want to dishonor Ba, either.

Worry buzzes in my belly, biting like mosquitoes. I remember Ba saying that Europeans visiting Africa had to take opium to sleep because of mosquitoes. Perhaps I should leave that out of my talk.

Grandmother Jones leaves me and heads over to talk with four visitors on the porch. They have to be visitors, because they aren't familiar, and they don't look like men I've seen around Pass Christian.

Two white men, two black men. No, I've not seen them before. Younger, maybe half Grandmother Jones's age—but they seem important. Worry lines crease their brows. Drag their cheeks down, and down. These are men accustomed to frowning. Men who have known hardship. And yet, they smile with my grandmother. And laugh.

She laughs, too, and her eyes shine like Ba's did when she was happy. I fight an urge to go stand beside her, just because I feel alone and out of place.

Would that help?

Instead, I linger near the door as the sun sets, watching people pass by into the long pew-filled sanctuary, with its floor-to-ceiling stained glass windows lining both walls. The congregation chats and whispers as people do when they have known each other a lifetime.

No one on earth has known me for a lifetime.

Maybe Clay will come soon with Miss Hattie. Or Gisele with Crazy Sardine, because even Crazy Sardine attends the Baptist Church.

Grandmother Jones leaves her companions and heads in through a side door near the front of the church, the altar, where the preacher will speak from his podium. Where the choir behind him will sing about Jesus and heaven.

She motions for me to follow. I glance at her face and catch a lingering moment of softness before the rocky lines come back. In the picture Clay has from six years ago, Grandmother Jones's expression looks like stone, as it does now. What does it really mean? Other than maybe I'm not her only trouble.

I study her from the side, but I don't think I'll ever be able to ask her.

We seat ourselves close to the front on the end of a pew, so I can stand up easily when it's my turn. I'll be able to turn around and talk almost like the preacher, with the choir behind me ready to sing about Jesus. Or heaven. Or something else loud and rhythmic and wonderful.

The mosquitoes in my belly turn to hornets, poking and stinging.

Someone taps me on the shoulder, and I wheel around to find Clay.

"Hey," he says, and gives me a smile. There's no sign of a problem with his neck, and he's not rubbing it anymore.

"Hey," I say, and smile back at him. I also smile at Miss Hattie-with-the-Amazon-face. She nods, and they sit in the pew behind me. When I turn my attention back to the front of the church, I see that the four visiting men Grandmother Jones spoke to have climbed the steps beside the altar and taken visitor's seats next to the pastor. Somehow they look even more important, up there in front of us, framed by the blue-robed choir.

Pastor Bickman mounts the steps and walks to his podium.

The church goes silent, except for kids fidgeting, the whish-whish of ceiling fans and hand fans, and the growing roar of crickets and frogs welcoming the darkness outside. I smell sweat and perfume. Oil and lotion.

Grandmother Jones draws a slow breath and lets it out. Her fingers shift against her knee. Tapping.

Is she worried about what I will say?

I am.

I've worked on my words a hundred times in my head, and a few times on paper. I even rehearsed once in front of Gisele. Clay listened only for a minute, then told me I was crazy and stalked off.

Nothing sounds right, no matter how hard I try.

Pastor Bickman opens our service. A prayer, and a song. He introduces our guests. Names I don't know.

"After the service," Pastor Bickman says, "Miss Jones, Miss Potts, and Miss Louis will meet with the representatives from the Freedom Democratic Committee, the Mississippi Teachers Association, and the Delta Ministry to finish plans for desegregating Pass Christian High School. We're trying hard to address the demotion of our principals to positions of no authority or mock authority at best."

Nervous shifting.

Some nods.

An "Mm-hmm" to my left.

"About time," from behind. "Don't want Principal Ellis ending up supervisor of janitors, like Principal Smith over at McComb."

I try to listen, but my mind sticks on the first thing the pastor said. Grandmother Jones is to meet with these visitors . . . to help with desegregation. . . .

*. . . And this fight, it's far from over, Ruba. I hope you realize you've landed in the middle of a battle bound to last your whole life. . . .*

Words from our earlier conversation echo like distant thunder. I squirm. A new set of mosquitoes takes flight in my belly, stinging me about the end of the month, when I must go to a Pass Christian school for the first time. A new fight. One I can't win with arrows or knives. No club or musket will see me through the first day of class in a Mississippi school.

The pastor goes on talking, about a committee to plan for possible riots or mobs.

Whether it would help or not, and even though I can't run fast, I wish I had a musket like my Amazon foremothers did back in the 1800s. Dahomey's war women pasted shells on their stocks for each enemy they killed.

"And now," Pastor Bickman announces, "the newest member of our congregation is ready to tell us her name and talk a little about herself. She'll even talk about where the struggle began, yes, Lord. Where it began. Stand up, Ruba. Give us some wisdom."

I feel dizzy. Sure I will fall. I use the bench in front of me to pull myself to my feet. Turn around. My throat dries and clenches as I look from face to face. Set of eager eyes to set of eager eyes.

They aren't as blank as I thought they'd be.

Is that good or bad?

I want to faint.

Someone waves from the back pew. A flash of brown between the dozens of cream-colored hand fans.

Gisele.

I see her leaning against Crazy Sardine's long arm. He's wearing a gold tunic and blue jeans, and his Afro is combed out as wide and tall as it will go. I've never seen anyone wear hair like that, and I wouldn't know what to call it if Clay hadn't told me. I can't help wondering if Crazy Sardine combed it out so big so people would stare at him more and me less.

He smiles. I smile back. Focusing on Gisele's small face, I begin.

"My name is Ruba Jones. I was born in Haiti. My Grandmother Ba—I mean, Ruba Cleo—taught me a lot. She taught me about weather and tides, shells and fish. She taught me about herbs and plants and trees and nature. She taught me to read and to write. She taught me the history of the world as she knew it, and the history of our family. We are the Fon people from the Kingdom of Dahomey, on the West African coast."

Gisele's smile seems to fill her whole face. I breathe to

slow my racing heart and continue. "In the old time, that coast was rain forest. Too thick for walking. Too thick for living, except a stretch of grassland now called the Gap of Benin. Around the time the *Mayflower* landed in America, the Fon people left Africa's beach and moved inland through the Gap of Benin. Ever after, Dahomey grew as this country did, almost a twin, rising to become an empire. On the backs of slaves."

Fans stop moving as hands freeze in place. Some people look angry. Others seem fascinated. Absorbed.

"While cotton grew in the United States, Dahomey grew bananas, pineapple, sugarcane, peanuts, yams, coffee—and yes, cotton, and more. All with the labor of slaves."

The angry people glare and glare. Pastor Bickman clears his throat. I clench my fists and force myself to continue. My throat feels so dry I'm scared I'll croak instead of talk.

"And later, the Fon built their capital city of Abomey, and inside the city, they made the great fortress of Simboji Palace. Kings ruled from Simboji with their advisers beside them, and fierce war women—my Amazon foremothers—guarded each gate. And even those strong black women had slaves."

I know Grandmother Jones has become a statue beside me. Granite or marble. Cold and unmoving. I hope she will let me finish. Her hand twitches, as if to inch toward mine. Words leave my mouth faster, and faster.

"Other African tribes built their empires. Oyo and Egba, and others. All traded in slaves. Black people, using each other for currency. Riches. Power. To gain what white men had to offer. Steel. Guns. Weapons. Better ways to kill each other. Better ways to live white men's lives. Or die too soon to enjoy them."

Crazy Sardine nods, and it gives me a spurt of energy.

"Only once in Dahomey did a king try to stop the slave trade. King Agaja was his name. He closed the slave ports. Some think he did it to gain control of the trade, but I think he disagreed with it. And I think he disagreed with letting other countries, other people, tell us what's right and wrong for us."

A few more fans stop moving. I blink fast to keep my eyes from watering.

"Agaja couldn't live forever, and his foolish son opened the slave ports again. And so, while this country fought its Civil War, Dahomey sold hundreds of slaves to the traders, and the foolish new king took even more for himself. This my grandmother Ruba Cleo taught me. Not so I would think less of Africa. Not so I would turn my back on my heritage. So I would remember what happened. Embrace it. And understand."

"Understand what, Sister?" Crazy Sardine's voice floats over the stunned faces like a welcome breeze.

"Understand how we almost saved ourselves, and how we tore ourselves apart. Understand that we first have to be loyal to each other, and stand together against those who would use us and kill us, and tell us what's right and what's wrong. Wherever we are, we have to live with the values of others, but keep our own. We need to live *black* lives even in a white world. With our own history. Our own traditions. Our own worth. We have to remember what came before guns and steel. It wasn't perfect, but it was *ours*. I'm Ruba Jones, daughter of Circe Cleo and James Howard Jones, and I remember."

"Amen," someone says.

My heart nearly stops.

That someone . . . it was Grandmother Jones. The very woman who has been telling me to let go of my past.

Her face looks tense and serious, but she is smiling. A real smile. For me.

My hands start shaking.

I realize Crazy Sardine is on his feet. Everyone is standing, and beginning to sing. Grandmother Jones stands, too, and she measures me with her gaze. Opens her arms—and glass explodes into the sanctuary.

Songs turn to screams.

Rocks thrown through the stained-glass windows

gouge the wall beside me.

People duck. Dodge. Drop to the floor. Clay, Gisele—I can't see them. My hand smacks my waist where my knife would be, if I were in Haiti.

Grandmother Jones pulls me down in front of her, between the first two pews. Pastor Bickman and the visiting men press against a wall and edge toward the door beside the altar. I can see them from under the pew, between the wooden braces.

Hoots and shouts rise outside.

"Y'all listen up in there," growls a voice I've heard once before. On a beach. Talking to his son.

"Listen up and listen nice. No interrupting."

Frye.

Leroy Frye.

# CHAPTER SEVEN

## Sunday, 10 August 1969: night

Pastor Bickman stands between us and the broken windows, his back to the sanctuary and his Bible in his hand, as if to shield us all. He shouts through the gaping holes in windows when he speaks. "We have no quarrel with you. Leave us in peace."

Through one of the broken windows, dead center in the jagged hole that once had been stained-glass doves and light from heaven, I can see someone out there on the wraparound porch. The height, the arrogant way he stands—I'm sure it's Leroy Frye in a sheet marked by a red and white cross on the breast. He pushes his hood back, showing me what I already knew.

Frye spits on the porch, slams his hand against the window frame, and laughs as the rest of the jagged glass tumbles ceiling to floor.

*He's made his own door now,* my mind gibbers.

"We got a quarrel with you, boy," Frye shouts back. "You and yours."

The choir, still together, rises to its feet. Eyes closed, they join hands.

"Oh, no," I hear Grandmother Jones whisper from behind me. "Please, God, no." Her hands hold my ankles. Squeeze my ankles. Tighter. Tighter.

"We went and got soft on local big-mouths like that Potts boy," Frye shouts. "Guess we should have paid more attention. He's been up to no good, and it's a damn shame. Forgot all his manners."

I hear engines. Motors. Cars or trucks. And many of them. Torches bob into view behind Leroy Frye. Hooded heads, and hooded eyes. Empty holes in the hot evening.

Miss Hattie shifts on the floor. She and Clay must have ducked down in the row behind ours. I can see their arms under the bench as Miss Hattie starts a wheezing chant. "Not my boy. You won't take my boy. Kill you first, God forgive me, but I'll kill you first. Not my boy. You won't take my boy. . . ."

"But really," Frye continues, "we got a bigger problem. And she's right in there. I can see her, crawling on the floor like a big fat ant. Her."

Leroy Frye leans through the broken window-door and points a dirty finger straight at me.

"We come about her. The juju gal. Send her out so we can have a look at a real A-freek-an witch."

Terror nearly melts me, but I have to try. These

people—my grandmother, my friends—they could get hurt because of me. I start to stand.

Grandmother Jones slams me to the floor. Covers me head to toe with her own body, breathing hard. I smell fear like sour onions on her breath. On her hand as it covers my mouth.

"Send her out or we'll burn her out," Frye says.

Even from the floorboards, I can see the torch in his hand, coming closer to the hole in the glass. And closer.

Grandmother Jones won't let me go. Won't let me move. I squirm and make like I can't breathe, and at least she frees my mouth. Turns loose some of my power.

"Do I need to start counting?" Frye asks.

Pastor Bickman mutters to the visitors.

"Let her up, Mrs. Jones," Clay says. "Ruba, she can take care of herself."

Let me up. Yes! Please, let me up.

"Ruba," Gisele says. "Rain on 'em, Ruba."

"One," says Leroy Frye. "Two."

And he throws his torch through the window.

I fill my lungs and chant as fast as I can, closing my eyes, rocking beneath my grandmother's weight.

She tries to keep me still.

I rock harder, moving her like a cork on water, chanting and chanting, once more calling on Circe, on Ba, and back, and back. Asking for guidance. Asking for help.

A breeze begins, rising behind the choir. I can see them through the pew's wooden floor braces still, and a few singers open their eyes. Others hum. Robes billow as the breeze swirls. The breeze shoots forward and snuffs the torch as it rolls across the floor, from dangerous fire to charred rags and a stick.

I keep chanting. The choir keeps humming. From the back of the church I hear Gisele giggle, and I think I hear her clap.

The breeze I called roars in a circle. Like a dust devil in the field. Like a swirl in fall leaves. It moves before me, dancing as I chant. On my command, it heads for Pastor Bickman.

His eyes widen, and he holds up his Bible.

The breeze knocks a wing from the broken stained-glass dove as it leaves the church through the gaping window—still obeying my will.

Leroy Frye steps toward the churning wind, bringing him square into my line of sight. He reaches out. Tries to touch the wind.

It bites at him like a dog. He leaps back, and that wind blows Leroy Frye right off the porch of Pass Christian Missionary Baptist Church.

I could use the wind to hurt him more. Even kill him. But I don't.

"A push," I murmur loud enough for my grandmother

to hear. "Not a shove."

Pastor Bickman and the visiting men turn in my direction. Slow. Like in a dream.

Grandmother Jones rolls off of me.

"Praise God. Praise Jesus," Miss Hattie says from the pew behind us.

"Told you she could take care of herself," Clay mumbles.

I can't read my grandmother's face. Even the lines are gone now. Slack, and vacant—like those people on the beach. Like I've become a haunt to her. A sea-shine, or something too filthy to see.

*You conjured in the house of God,* I imagine her thinking. I imagine her rage, building slow like the stormwitch's spells on the ocean.

*Witch. Witch!*

Broken stained glass in the rest of the windows turns loose and shatters on the church floor.

From outside, angry voices begin rising once more.

I scramble to my feet and run out the front door onto the church's porch, no longer caring at all what happens to me.

Gisele and Crazy Sardine run out behind me, and Gisele manages to grab my hand. I stop, but keep my face away from her. I hate that I'm crying. I hate that the foul men in sheets might see my tears.

Leroy Frye strides toward me, past a line of cars and more cars and sheet-men holding torches. He stops beside a pickup where three shorter sheets are standing in the bed.

"Ray-boy, Poke, and Dave Allen," I say, turning loose the anger I held for the sake of my grandmother. "Why do you play at this foolishness?"

"Foolishness," Gisele says, and she laughs. "Fools."

Leroy Frye's face goes the color of blood and turnips. "Y'all shut your mouths. And you, Juju, my boy said you did a witch curse in the woods. He says you poured some water on his head."

"Your boy's been in the sun too long," mutters Crazy Sardine, and I almost smile.

"She doesn't do witch curses," says Clay, elbowing past Crazy Sardine. Miss Hattie is right behind him, snatching at his shoulder. "No such thing as witches. Don't they teach you that in church?"

"You calling me a liar, boy?" Frye growls. One car door opens behind him. And another, and another. His friends in sheets are coming out to play.

"Yeah," says Gisele. "He's callin' you a liar, 'cause you are a liar. Ruba doesn't do witch curses. She does witch dances."

Frye laughs. A grating sound.

"You're about little enough to eat," he says to Gisele.

"Damn shame pickaninny meat's always so stringy."

The other sheets close in, torches hot and crackling.

My muscles tense and my eyes narrow. I focus on the fire. I let the faces of my foremothers burn angry in my mind, and I step forward.

"Your boy tried to lynch Clay with a belt today, over in the trees near the campground," I say. Too loud. And it feels good.

"You got a big mouth." Leroy Frye spits in my direction, but before it even leaves his lips, I touch my lips with two fingers and blow.

His stream of tobacco juice turns in midair and spatters back at his feet. He stares at it.

"Told you, Daddy," whines Ray-boy from under his pointed hood. I would know his voice anywhere now.

"Why did you come in sheets?" I take another step forward, toward the pickup where the three boys have started to fidget under their disguises. "What are you afraid of?"

I raise my hand, and a burst of the lingering wind snuffs the torch closest to me. The man holding it lets out a curse and shakes the smoldering stick.

I snap my fingers three times.

Three more torches go dark.

More swearing. Some shouts.

"Daddy, make her stop!" Ray-boy insists.

I spread my arms and blow air like I'm throwing up all over Ray-boy and his friends.

All the torches are extinguished.

The crowd mutters.

People shove through the doorway behind me, but I don't change my position. With my arms up, I'm ready to act. I'm getting tired fast, though. Only three weeks, and already I'm out of practice.

In front of me, a sheet-man with a rifle rushes forward. Again I vomit wind on Ray-boy and let it spread as far as it'll go. The rifle rips from the man's hands and sails into a tree. It fires, and men in sheets scurry like raccoons in a lightning burst.

Car doors slam. Pickup doors slam.

Engines crank.

Ray-boy and his friends leap from the truck bed and run.

In moments, it's just me and Leroy Frye, face to face in the almost-darkness.

"Ain't we the big shot." He spits.

Hands still in the air, lips puckered, I blow his spit back at him again. This time, it lands on his shirt.

He brushes the juice away without taking his eyes from me. "Gonna have to teach you a lesson."

Clay steps forward and stands next to me. "Teach us both, then."

Frye sneers at Clay.

Crazy Sardine comes next. "And me."

Miss Hattie—stern Amazon glare full in place—appears at my shoulder. "And me."

And the women come, in hats and dresses, carrying their white gloves in their hands.

And the men in suits and ties, all shaved and scrubbed.

And the little boys, with chins out, acting big.

And the little girls in dyed cotton, tugging bright ribbons that match their socks.

The whole church, save for Grandmother Jones and Pastor Bickman, presses Leroy Frye toward his truck.

"You're just one man," I say. "One man dressed in a bedsheet. You want me afraid of you?"

Leroy Frye's face becomes a dark, puffed scowl. His eyes flash and stab.

We don't move.

He turns his back as if he's not afraid, but jumps into the cab of his truck in a hurry.

We hold our ground without a twitch. Without a murmur.

Leroy Frye cranks his engine. He sits and squeezes his steering wheel for a few seconds, then roars away, spinning dust in our faces.

Clay lets out a nervous laugh as Frye clears the church

parking lot and careers off down the road. His mother laughs, too, and Crazy Sardine taps one platform heel to the other.

From the porch, I hear sobbing from Grandmother Jones. "God be with us," she whispers. "There'll be a war now, for sure."

*13 August 1969*

*Dearest Ba,*

*For the smallest moment, I thought Grandmother Jones might be proud of me. Three days ago, after I spoke in the church—before the white men came—I felt like we were starting to understand each other and get along. I thought she might come to trust me, or at least respect what I've been taught. I would have given my life for her last Sunday night. For her and my cousin, and my new friends.*

*But after those men came and I fought with them . . . well, Grandmother Jones and I got right back to fighting. She refused to look at me on the drive home. Once we got here, she swore if I use my magic again, she will have no more of me. She said my spells are the devil's work, and I would have to leave her home.*

*I was so upset I couldn't even write you.*

*The next day, I told her we serve the same Creator. I told her if she'd only trust me, my magic might save us when the storm-witch's spirit comes ashore.*

*The walls rattled when Grandmother Jones slammed my bedroom door.*

*I've been grounded to my room since then.*

*Perhaps the evil in the hurricane will be an easier adversary than Grandmother Jones.*

*Clay, Gisele, and Crazy Sardine—they come by and try to make me smile, and lots of times, they do. Gisele has midnight skin, dark as mine, and her hair feels strong like a snake rope. And there is something in her eyes. Even her laugh. I think the wind knows Gisele, Ba.*

*I think Gisele is like me. That she could be an Amazon one day.*

*But how will I train her? I feel like I know so little. And what if I make a mistake and lose her to the stormwitch like I lost you?*

*I still don't recall all of what happened when you died, my grandmother. Though I try in each dream. I reach with each stray thought.*

*All I want is to come home, to stand with you and raise our hands to the wind, and see in your eyes how much you care. Your face always told me all I needed to know of what was in your heart.*

*I can't believe you're gone.*

*I can't believe I let you go.*

# CHAPTER EIGHT

## Friday, 15 August 1969: Morning

"A few days ago, when we spoke of pushing instead of shoving, you mentioned local people like Mrs. Fannie Lou Hamer and Mr. Guyot." I eat country ham and biscuits before Grandmother Jones goes to work. I'm up early to please her on the first day after my grounding is over. "Where do you know them from?"

"Everybody around here knows Fannie Lou Hamer," Grandmother Jones says. "She's from up around Ruleville, and she got arrested and beaten over wanting to vote. Lost her job. But she rose over it all and led us with the power of her voice. The force of her soul. Lord, but if you could hear her speak, Ruba. And sing. With all she's been through—I would have followed Mrs. Hamer into hell and believed I could come out alive. Guess that's what we did, now that I think on it."

I don't speak because she might stop if I interrupt her.

"And Lawrence Guyot," she continues. "He organized most of Pass Christian's local efforts. We worked together during Freedom Summer."

"But I thought you didn't agree with the people who came down for Freedom Summer." I cover my mouth. The thought popped out even as I tried to grab it.

Grandmother Jones frowns around a mouthful of strawberry jam. "I didn't, but once we all started working, I did my part."

Her part. I think of Clay's photo. Grandmother Jones probably marched with marchers and gathered at the gatherings.

Before I can ask, she says, "I helped teach colored—no, no, I promised Hattie yesterday I'd try to say *black,* at least amongst our own folks—anyway, I taught black history over at the Gulfport Freedom School. And I kept some CORE volunteers here at the house. CORE covered the Gulf Coast during the registration effort. Hattie kept a bunch of those kids, too."

"Here? Freedom Summer volunteers stayed in this house?" I load my plate again, hoping Grandmother Jones will keep talking. "But Clay said people who kept volunteers . . ."

"Got beaten. Yes, they did. But I was lucky. We took a few bullets and some rocks through the window—one with a burning rag on it." Grandmother Jones nods toward the front window, but my eyes search the wall behind her. Are there bullet holes beneath my father's picture? Beside the bookshelf?

Grandmother Jones might have patched them. Yes, she probably painted over the pain and hid the scars of survival.

"Hattie got beaten twice, though," Grandmother Jones says. "With hose pipe. Kluxers like the hose pipe because it doesn't leave evidence. Over at the Freedom School, several of our kids got taken and whipped on their way home."

"Did—did any of them die?"

"Not that summer, Ruba. The coast, we always had it a little easier because of the tourists and the military bases and all. It's more liberal down here than upstate. Julian Bond—he was the Student Nonviolent Coordinating Committee's communications director—he reckons that around eighty people got beaten during Freedom Summer. Four died, and four got hurt bad. A thousand or so got arrested, and then there were bombings. More over in Amite County than here—but all together, thirty-seven churches and thirty black-owned businesses or homes got hit."

All of that, in three months. I make myself eat another bite of biscuit and try to pretend my belly's not running out of room. "But why don't you talk about it?" I ask. "Talk about it all the time, all the brave things you did?"

"It hurts, for one thing. I think of all the good, and all

the problems. But what I did wasn't anything special, child. Nothing every person around me didn't do, every day. Every single day. Some of them have been doing it for years—and some of them are still working just as hard. Let them talk about it all the time. They deserve the credit."

Grandmother Jones finishes her country ham and goes to rinse her plate at the sink. She seems more relaxed this morning. Even a little friendly.

"Clay and I want to go to Blankenship's today," I say. "And to the beaches. But we won't make trouble, any more than what comes from just being there. We only want to have a soda and walk."

"You have no business being anywhere risky after what you did to Leroy Frye. You have no business out of this yard, Ruba."

I see Grandmother Jones's shoulders stiffen, and I know I've made another mistake. With nothing to lose, I plunge ahead. "Why do you try to keep me prisoner here? I'm sixteen years old, and in Haiti I took care of Ba. I took care of myself."

Silence answers me.

I drop my eyes, confused. My chest aches. I'm so sick of not knowing what to say. How to act.

Grandmother Jones comes and pats my hand. "I know I've been strict with you. I've tried to be extra careful because you've lost so much, and with your accent and your foreign ways—well, I figured you'd rain trouble on your own head. And you have."

"Mississippi is my place now, at least for a time. Why shouldn't I fight like you did, to make it better?"

Something like understanding weights Grandmother Jones's voice as she says, "When all's said and done, I know you'll fight, no matter how I feel about it. Thing is, I don't want you hurt, Ruba. I—I don't think I could stand that."

Tears streak down Grandmother Jones's cheeks. She looks worried, like someone who has seen many terrible things she would like me not to see. I lift my arms, and she leans down. Lets me hug her neck. Her hair smells of powder and the ham she cooked for my breakfast.

When we move apart, Grandmother Jones lifts her apron and dries her face, and leaves without a word.

The warmth from her hug lingers even as the sound of her car's engine fades.

I get up, holding my hand to my cheek, and face the window.

Bullets came in through that glass, Grandmother Jones said.

I turn to the wall. Walk up to it.

And I see them immediately.

How could I've missed them? Right there, between

and under pictures, level with my neck and head.

Five bullet holes, in a jagged line.

If I had been here then . . . if any of them had been standing in front of that window . . .

On close inspection, I see the bullet holes have been smoothed but left as a part of the wood. Each one has a cross sketched next to it, and the same date. As if someone simply accepted such a risk, wanted to make a record—and knew more bullets might come.

I touch the holes, feeling frozen and hot all at once.

Holes made by hatred, in a wall so solid I can't imagine it falling, no matter the loose nails and creaking supports.

Grandmother Jones's rock face makes sense to me now. It's not hatred or lack of feeling, anger, or even distress.

My grandmother wears the stern expression of a warrior, simple as that.

# CHAPTER NINE

## Friday, 15 August 1969: Afternoon

Clay, Gisele, and I again walk the white-only beach. Most people ignore us, but a few take the time to glare. My journal's in my pocket, but today I don't feel like I have to touch it every few seconds to stay alive.

"You hear any more about that storm on the way?" Gisele asks. "Daddy says it's getting worse."

"No," I say.

Clay only snorts. He doesn't seem concerned. I'm learning that Clay pays attention to the Panthers and the television, national news and music. The rest he ignores.

Near a lifeguard stand, a young white boy with freckles on his face, maybe five or six years old, lets me put my ear to his radio and listen for the weather report. When his mother sees, she screams and chases us away with handfuls of sand.

We ease away from her and keep on walking.

She rants and swears behind us. We continue without looking back or changing our strides. Pushing, not shoving, I tell myself.

"Get used to us," Clay mutters every now and then. "You folks better get used to us."

Gisele does a lot of skipping, sometimes throwing up sand and trying to blow it away before it hits her face. She doesn't seem to care if anyone gets used to us or not.

We walk all the way to Blankenship's. No one is at the soda counter when we sit down. Still, the man at the register glares when we place our order.

"Thank you," Clay says when the man brings our drinks—in paper cups, the kind we're supposed to take and leave.

The man slams the first drink down in front of me so hard I'm surprised the cup isn't crushed. Soda sloshes on the counter. He does it again in front of Clay, and a third time in front of Gisele.

I smile and wipe up the spills, never taking my eyes from his. My refusal to look down seems to make him madder than anything, and he storms off to clean a milk-shake machine.

We take our sodas out of the drugstore without sitting at the counter and head over to Gisele and Crazy Sardine's back porch. In that private place, screened in to keep out mosquitoes, we relax. We even listen to a radio no one will scream and throw sand at us over, or snatch away. The Four Tops sing "It's the Same Old Song," and

I tap my foot.

Grandmother Jones comes home from work. When she glances in our direction, I wave. She gives me a flip of her hand. Soon, I should go and help her with dinner, but the afternoon feels warm and lazy.

Gisele plays quietly by herself, and I can't help noticing her doll is white. I tell her I plan to make her a Haitian doll, and some proper fetishes, too.

"You should see your own black face in your dolls, just like in the mirror–and be proud," I say.

"Right on, Sister." Clay tilts back in his rickety wooden chair and glances at cloudy skies.

The song ends.

"Motown's finest," the announcer says. "And what about that weather? Gonna have rain today along the Gulf, our first gift from Tropical Storm Camille. She may be a hurricane soon, and she's heading for Cuba."

The announcer moves on to other news, then introduces Martha and the Vandellas. "Nowhere to Run."

I'm not sure I like that title.

"You ever been to Cuba?" Clay asks.

"Cuba Ruba," Gisele says. "Cuba Ruba gonna get herself a tuba." She giggles.

"I've been to Cuba," I say. "Ba took me to the markets. It's a crowded place."

"You see Fidel Castro?" Clay asks.

I laugh. "You're funny, Clay. Castro's face is everywhere in Cuba."

"Daddy says President Kennedy tried to blow Castro away, Cuba Ruba," Gisele says.

"I know." I sigh. "In Haiti, we have Papa Doc. People either love or hate men like Castro and Papa Doc, Ba said. She also said a country's business is their own."

"Who's Papa Doc?" Clay asks.

"François Duvalier, Haiti's president. Say a word against him, and the Tontons Macoutes take you away."

"The Tonton-what?" Gisele swats a fly on her arm.

"Papa Doc's police," I say. "The police in Haiti work for the president."

"Sounds more like a king than a president," Clay mutters.

I shrug. "He's president to us, or he was. When I came here, he was sick. Probably his son will take over soon."

"Cops around here, they aren't always honest, either," Clay says. "Leastwise not for black folks. Even with the Movement and all, it's real easy for us to disappear. Turn up lynched, or floating in the swamps."

"Tonton Macoutes." I shiver. "You disappear in Haiti, nobody finds you. But Papa Doc's strongmen never pestered Ba."

I don't say that even military police feared the war women, the storm chanters. Most people stayed far, far from our stretch of beach.

"Glad there ain't no Tontons 'round here," Gisele says, but a siren rises in the distance before she finishes her sentence.

We stop talking. Clay turns down the radio.

The siren creeps closer. And closer.

Clay straightens. I hug myself with shaking arms.

Gisele drops her doll. "If they coming after us, I don't wanna disappear."

"They aren't coming after us," Clay says.

But the siren, it's coming closer still. Nearby now.

"We're only children," I tell Gisele.

"Doesn't matter," Clay says. "A five-year-old boy got put in jail over in McComb. For waving an American flag at a trooper."

"Don't scare Gisele," I say. "Meanness helps nothing."

"I'm telling the truth!" Clay jumps up and glares at me. "That boy was only five."

The siren turns down our dead-end road. Flashing lights make the screened porch flicker blue.

"Clay, why are they comin' here?" Gisele asks.

My heart pounds. I think of my war clothes. My bow and arrows—all hidden in my room at Grandmother Jones's next door. But she's home. I could never get them out without her seeing, and I don't think I could stand making her angry. At least I have my journal.

Clay grabs my hand. "Come on. Let's get out of here. Hide. Hide!"

He opens the screen door and darts out, pulling me along with him. Gisele follows, clinging to her white doll. We slip behind trees and bushes until we have a good view of the police cruiser.

The cruiser's siren wails. Its blue lights twirl and flash as it pulls slowly into Grandmother Jones's driveway.

We watch behind curtains of hanging moss and vines as Grandmother Jones answers the side door to a young white man in a black uniform.

I see her sag when she greets him, like she's tired. But I know the truth, from her own words. Grandmother Jones is afraid. Immediately, I don't like the policeman.

"What can I do for you, Officer Bolin?" Grandmother Jones asks.

The officer removes his hat, uncovering dark bristles of hair. "Sorry to trouble you, Maizie. I'm looking for your granddaughter and her friend Clay Potts."

"Maizie," Clay grumbles. "Bet if I called his grandmother by her first name without permission, he'd slap me silly."

I wonder if I can slap the officer and run fast enough to avoid capture. Would that be a push or a shove?

"What do you want with them, if you don't mind me asking?" Grandmother Jones's eyes have gone wide. She stands straighter now. Tense, and wary.

"I need to ask them some questions, Maizie."

"We don't make trouble, Officer. Ruba didn't make trouble on purpose. She's not from here, you know. She's learning."

In my mind, I see the officer as a growling dog, challenging a mother with a pup. I see my grandmother rolling over and exposing her belly. Submitting, with her downcast eyes and calm words.

"I didn't figure her for too much of a troublemaker," Officer Bolin allows. "Kid stuff, really, because she's hanging around with Clay Potts and all his loud-mouth ideas. But Mrs. Mack says Clay, Ruba, and Gisele stole her radio at the white-only beach today."

I cut my eyes to Clay, who turns up a palm. We don't know a Mrs. Mack, and we didn't take any radio. I think about the freckle-faced boy and the woman who hit us with sand, and just then Grandmother Jones speaks.

"Is this some meanness from Leroy Frye?" Grandmother Jones asks, still in her quiet, submissive voice. "Mrs. Mack's mighty good friends with him, and he's angry with Ruba."

Officer Bolin doesn't react except to say, "Will you bring those children to me when they come home? I need to clear this up."

A moment's silence, and then Grandmother Jones

flaps her apron once. To the side. In our direction, as if to say, "Shoo. Get out of here."

She turns her back to us without a glance. A cloud of flour dust from her apron sprinkles the ground near the policeman. "Of course," she says. "As soon as I finish cooking, I'll go find them, so justice can roll down like water. Would that satisfy you?"

I gasp, recognizing my grandmother's play on words. From Dr. Martin Luther King's *"I have a dream"* speech, that she reads aloud at least once a week.

*"When will you be satisfied? We can never be satisfied as long as our bodies, heavy with the fatigue of travel, cannot gain lodging in the motels of the highways and the hotels of the cities . . . No, no, we are not satisfied . . ."*

The officer seems clueless about this little jab. He just nods his head and walks back to his car.

Clay punches my shoulder. "Come on, Ruba. Let's get out of here."

# CHAPTER TEN

## Friday, 15 August 1969: night

We ease away from our hiding place in the bushes behind Gisele's house as the officer climbs into his car. Rain mists as we run deeper into thickets of vines and trees. We're heading away from the main road and the beaches, leaving behind the sounds of waves and engines.

Clay leads the way down dirt paths and occasional side streets, half a mile, then maybe a mile. We slip around board homes and through hedges. We even pass a few white-columned mansions. They seem misplaced so far away from the sand and brilliant ocean views.

Gisele takes three steps to my two, but she keeps pace. Clay leads the way without looking back.

"Where are we going?" I ask.

"I don't know!" Clay's head turns from side to side, as if searching for a good hiding place. "Over toward the shipyards? We can wait in the trees until after dark."

A warm smatter of rain hits my nose. "Good as any, I suppose."

We dodge cars and trees until we reach the woods near the shipping docks. This far back from the beach, two miles at least, the coast is more marshland than forest. Waterlogged banks and soggy trenches stretch as far as I can see, and cypress knees—the roots—lift like reddish-brown warts above the brackish surface.

Clay and I settle on the solid ground between two trenches while Gisele tries to collect two green horse-apples from a Bodark tree's low-slung branches. *Osage orange* is what they call that thorny, thorny tree in reference books, but I know it now by its Mississippi name. Gisele isn't afraid of the thorns at all. She hops and grabs until she gets what she wants, then bounces back to us, drops on her knees, and starts rolling the horse-apples back and forth to me.

I stretch forward to catch one, and she gasps.

"Why you got a alligator on your leg?" Gisele points, and I startle as I realize my cotton dress has scooted up to show part of my thigh. My Amazon tattoo shines like a blue light on my dark skin.

"It's a crocodile," I tell her, snapping my hands near her face. "Jaws stronger than rock, and white daggers for teeth. All Dahomey Amazons wore this mark."

Clay turns to look at me, leans forward staring at the tattoo, and for the first time ever, he makes as if to touch me. I barely see the movement of his finger as it stretches toward my thigh.

I react with no thought. Grab. Twist. Push. Hold.

In seconds, Clay lies on his back, a victim of my long years of training.

He coughs. Catches his breath. "Dang, Ruba! Get off me!"

I jerk my hand from his throat and sit back. "I—I—am sorry. Please, don't touch me."

"Don't worry about that, ever again!" Clay jumps to his feet and sulks away to sit by a marshy puddle.

Gisele watches him splash the water, and she giggles. "How did you throw him over so easily?"

I gaze into her bright young eyes, and something stirs in my belly. She really wants to know. I can tell by the way her eyes shine. "Like this," I say, and I show her by taking her arm and using my weight and position as leverage.

Grab. Twist. Push. Hold.

She gets back up immediately and grabs my arm to practice, and I feel the strength in her hands as she twists and pushes. I don't fall the first time, or the second. Not even the third.

On her fourth try, she tips me backward and drops down to grab my throat.

"Can I be a witch like you?" she begs as she lets me up.

Clay throws a look over his shoulder as I answer. "Yes, little sister. If you learn your foremothers and your history, and if you trust me. Trust is everything between war women, and between kings and their protectors."

"Why did the kings want women to protect them anyways?" Gisele asks.

"In Dahomey, many men died from wars with other tribes and nations, so the king didn't have enough to guard him and make his army, too. And most kings thought women were more loyal, more honest. They didn't let other men stay in the palace after dark. Only women, their advisers and protectors."

"Daddy told me about Amazons from Greece or South America somewhere. He never mentioned any African Amazons." She sits back and chews at her fingernail.

I grin. "British explorers called us Amazons, after the myths. And they are myths. Ba told me those other Amazons are legends—so we're the only real ones. The whites didn't know what to make of us, especially when they saw us fight, so they gave us the only name they had for powerful women. Now, see those thorns on that tree?"

Gisele glances where I point, toward the Bodark limbs. Long thorns. Some bigger than the finger I use to indicate them. She nods.

"African kings planted thorny vines like those branches around their palaces. Thorns that large, and larger. In battle, Amazon women ran at those branches and climbed over without slowing down."

Gisele swallows, staring at the thorns. "I don't think I could do that."

"You could with training. Amazons trained all day every day. And they fought. So fierce. So strong! When King Gezo took over, he could not kill the man he stole the throne from, because the old king's protectors were too strong. King Gezo had to keep the old king in a building on the palace grounds, and send him food. And that old king lived longer than Gezo!"

Gisele laughs. "Serves Geezer right, stealing thrones."

Clay wanders back from his puddle and plops down between us. "Y'all still talking about silly witch stuff?"

"You the one silly," Gisele says with a wave. "Ruba's talking 'bout the African war women."

Clay wrinkles his nose. "She's just saying that. Aren't you, Ruba? It's stories to scare people, like old slave tales about boogies and ghosts."

"The Amazons are real," I tell him. "I'm the last. The French killed all the rest in a war. I guard the spirit and memory of King Agaja, who tried to save Dahomey by closing the slave ports. I hope he'll help me fight the evil of the stormwitch Zashar, who won't keep herself in the land of the dead."

"Stupid," Clay said. "There's no such thing as spirits, except in Heaven. And no such thing as witches anywhere."

I clench one fist and chew my lip. Our beliefs sound foolish when he says those things. But they aren't foolish. My throat feels tight. I won't believe they're stupid or silly or wrong. I can't.

No.

What Ba taught me, all Ba knew—there's nothing foolish about those things, at least not to me.

"There wasn't any such thing as Black Power a few years back," I tell him. The words sound choked. "But people believed, and it's real now."

Clay looks a little guilty. He shrugs.

"King Agaja has a special spirit," I tell him, working hard not to grind my teeth and make my head hurt. "He lives on to protect Dahomey's descendants."

"Why does Aka-jo need to protect us?" Gisele asks.

"Because his son reopened the slave ports." I draw a line in the mud with my finger and make dots on each side. "Think about it this way. On this side of the line, there was Agaja's tradition and the Amazons who were my foremothers, including Tata."

Gisele nods. Clay grumbles something I can't hear.

"On this other side, there was Agaja's bad son and his stormwitch Zashar. They fought against my foremothers, and didn't honor Agaja's beliefs and traditions. So, the people on our side of the line got killed."

I rub out all the dots on our side, except one. "This dot

is Tata. She got thrown in the ocean and ended up on the island of Haiti."

Then I rub out all the dots on the other side except one. "All of these people got killed, too, because the slave trade made Dahomey weak, and other African nations, and the whites, especially the French, tore it apart. This dot, Zashar the stormwitch, watched her king fail, and she watched her country die. She started to hate white people, and she hated my foremothers, too, for being right about what would happen if those ports got opened again."

I rub out the last dot. "Then Zashar died, too, only her spirit isn't at peace."

"Ruba—" Clay begins, but Gisele cuts him off by popping his thigh with her hand.

I rub out all the lines and dots, make a new line, and put a rock on either side. "Now there's just Zashar's evil spirit." I point to one rock. "And me, the last Amazon." I point to the other rock. "Zashar uses her magic to send spirits into storms, trying to kill my family and me, and trying to kill white people. It's her revenge for slavery, and for the ruin of Dahomey and her king."

Real fast, I pick up both rocks and bash them together. Gisele jumps. Clay jumps, too, but he tries to act like he didn't.

"I have to fight her magic to save my life, and to save

innocent people. I have to send the spirits back to the land of the dead, so hurricanes will be just hurricanes, and not do any more damage than they have to." I put one rock down and smash it with the other, two hard blows, until it breaks into three or four pieces. "One day, I'll fight Zashar herself and beat her, I hope."

"There'll be one rock then," Gisele says as I place the stone that's still whole in front of her dusky folded legs. "And no evil in the storms."

"Right. Zashar will be finished, and the Amazon spirits can rest in peace." I smile at her. "And I can train a few new Amazons, to keep our history alive."

"I never heard such stupidness," Clay growls. "You're scaring the child."

I ignore him and focus on Gisele. "Boys have no soul for these things. Don't mind him. After she came to this side of the world, to Haiti, Tata guarded Agaja's spirit and beliefs to her grave, as was her sacred duty, sworn as a girl no older than you. So it's up to you, believe or don't, Gisele, but out on the sea–the storm is coming this way, and Zashar the stormwitch is using her magic to make it worse. If you listen, you'll hear the evil inside the wind sooner or later."

"It's a tropical storm," Clay argues. "It's weather. Science! Not magic. It's a hurricane, maybe, and it probably won't hit us."

"It will hit." I keep my voice even despite nervous twists in my belly. "And when it does, it's my job to turn the evil back, so the storm is just the storm nature intended. Otherwise, I might die, and lots of people who never did wrong to anyone might die with me."

*But what if* I'm *wrong?*

*What if Clay's right and I* am *imagining things?*

*No. No! I know what I know, and his doubts can't change what I know is real.*

"The storm's coming," I say again, stronger, with a little less worry. "It'll hit here and not long from now, and Zashar's dark magic will destroy us all if you don't trust me."

Clay wipes his forehead with his shirt, then lies back on the ground. "I believe you're some kind of witch, Ruba, because I saw what you can do. But I'm not believing some bad ghost is strolling across the ocean, all the way from Africa, because some dead black Amazon worked a spell and put that spirit in the wind to do evil. I'm going to sleep."

"We gonna spend the night here beside the shipyards?" Gisele asks him.

"Yeah," Clay says. He hugs himself and rolls over. "I'm not going home to get arrested. Maybe by tomorrow, Officer Bolin won't be thinking about us."

Gisele shrugs. She questions me about Haiti and

Africa until it's so dark we can't see each other, and finally falls asleep in my lap, her head resting on the journal in my pocket. It's a comforting feeling, the book against my crocodile tattoo, and the slight weight of Gisele as she dreams.

I sit, eyes wide, protecting what's mine.

Her breathing is slight, like a bird. Like a little crow. Ba had great respect for crows. Said they were as smart as monkeys. Crows defend their young with a fierceness like our own, and they have big families. When a crow dies, other crows mourn. I suppose crows see those holes in the sky, where stars should be. They miss their grandmothers like I miss Ba.

I feel tired. Of fighting. Of losing. Of thinking about dead people more than live people. I'm even tired of being mad, but I keep right on feeling that way. Part of me wants to relax, fall asleep, and wake up believing in Grandmother Jones's peace, that violence is like Dr. King said, "impractical and immoral."

The other part of me, maybe the part that still belongs to Ba and Dahomey and the Amazons, likes what Clay quotes, from Malcolm X. *A Negro is within his rights to use any method to remove these injustices for racial discrimination.*

Gisele stirs in my lap, and I hug her to me, sad that her mother's dead. If I had been there when she died in a Civil Rights march, I would have wanted to use any method to remove her killer. To right that injustice. But Gisele is alive, and so is her father. Nonviolence won at least that victory. Perhaps Crazy Sardine might have been killed—and Grandmother Jones, too—if they had shoved instead of pushed. I might have had no family left at all.

Then again, if they had used "any method," I might be living in a Mississippi with more proud black leaders like Malcolm X. Gisele might have a black doll instead of a white one if the protesters had been more militant. If they had fought like Amazons. But, when the Amazons met the French Legionnaires in 1892, it didn't matter who the better warriors were. The French had better weapons, and the Amazons died.

My belly twists again.

Perhaps I will do as my foremothers did. Shave my head, file my teeth to points, soak my nails in brine until they turn to spikes, and slay as many of the enemy as I can find. Show the white man Africa's woman heart. Make men like Leroy Frye understand that we're warriors, and we haven't been broken. Ba would be proud, but Grandmother Jones would be crushed.

*A battle bound to last my whole life . . .* That's what Grandmother Jones told me. I think of the bullet holes in her wall. Bile surges up my throat, and I cover my mouth.

It rains and rains. Soft, warm water, keeping the

clearing damp and chasing away the bugs—but chills run through me. I feel so wet. So uncomfortable and stiff. Sometimes I sway with sleep, but I always snap back to alertness. My muscles ache.

The hours stretch and stretch until the rain ends. Only then do I dare to take my journal from its dry place in my pocket. I'm grateful I have the book to keep me company.

*16 August 1969*

*Dearest Ba,*

*I'm in the marshes near a shipyard, hiding from American police. I'll have to face them soon, and I don't know what will happen.*

*The morning moves unquiet around us, Clay, Gisele, and me. At sunrise, I heard whispers in the wind. For a moment, they filled the air and rattled my spirit. The storm is moving fast now, almost here—but I've never heard anything like it.*

*Loud, bellowing wind.*

*And the voice inside, it's colder than any we've dealt with before.*

*Soon, I'll have to go home no matter what. I have to get my bow, my oils . . . so many things to gather! I have to be ready to fight the evil in this storm. Every time I look at Gisele or Clay, or think about Grandmother Jones and Crazy Sardine—I know I have to protect them. I can't let them be killed because the stormwitch is sending a spirit after me.*

*I think Gisele feels the winds, but without you I don't know if I should train her. Yet, if I don't train anyone, and I die right away, who will guard the memory of King Agaja and speak for our history?*

*Listen, Ba. Listen to the moaning whirlwind in the sea. I may fall, just as you did. Your hand, it rested wet in mine, and so slippery! I couldn't grip it. I couldn't hold when you needed me.*

*Sometimes I have a flash, the tiniest glimpse of that moment your fingers left mine.*

*Lightning in your hair . . . thunder in Agontime's footsteps far away, thunder in Agontime's words . . . rain . . . so much rain and wind . . .*

*Why did you start smiling?*

*What did you say?*

*Zashar's storm is coming, and I need to know.*

*The hurricane's coming, Ba.*

# CHAPTER ELEVEN

## Saturday, 16 August 1969: Morning

"Wake up, girl." I shake Gisele's shoulder.

She squints at me with sleepy young eyes and wipes her nose. "What do you want? I barely been sleeping, it's so noisy out here."

I eye Clay. He snores in the drizzle, and sometimes he coughs.

I don't think he can hear Camille's winds yet. I don't think anyone with normal ears can hear her.

But Gisele said it was noisy. My gaze turns back to her.

Can she hear the hurricane coming?

Gray half-light through tree fingers tells me Grandmother Jones has left for work, and I know she will be worried. We should go—but I can't ignore what Gisele said. "Is it still noisy to you?"

She shrugs. "Yeah."

"Tell me what you hear."

"Clay snoring . . . and rain dropping . . . and leaves swishing. . . ." She rubs her ears. "And some lady yelling about killin' people for good and ever."

Fear and joy blend inside me at once.

She hears the witch! Gisele *is* born to be an Amazon like me. I feel like frozen fire, hot and cold.

And yet, she could have had a dream, couldn't she? "This lady who's yelling, do you understand what she's saying?"

"Not really." Gisele yawns. "She sings, and she swears, and she yells crazy. Real loud, and there's back-and-forth shoos-shoos, and sometimes a splat."

"I think you're hearing the waves in front of the storm," I murmur. "And the spirit inside it, too. You're hearing her better than me."

Clay's eyes fly open. "You're crazy, Ruba." He pulls himself to his feet, shaking his head. "How could she be hearing something so far away? Spirit inside it—I swear, you're touched in the head."

Fast anger overtakes me, and I want to hit him. And then I want to cry. Maybe Gisele *did* just have a dream. Maybe I *am* just scaring her.

"Come on, Gisele. I'll take you home." Clay grabs at her hand, and Gisele doesn't hesitate.

Grab. Twist. Push. Hold.

She throws him to the ground, using her weight and position as leverage, just as I taught her the night before.

Clay props himself up on his elbows, groans, then

regards me from his backside like I've grown wings behind my ears. "This is your fault, Ruba!"

Gisele scratches her forehead as if she didn't just throw down a boy nearly three times her age. "Why? You're the one who touched me when I didn't ask you to."

Clay scrambles up, gives us a final scowl, and stalks off into the bushes. Gisele and I wait for a second, then not knowing what else to do, follow as he stomps through the trees.

He doesn't speak as we follow the path we took yesterday, beside misplaced mansions and through yards and past shacks until we near our dead-end street.

"The Man gonna get you," Gisele warns Clay as we turn for home. "Grandma Jones told that cop she would bring us to him, remember?"

"For what?" he asks, almost shouting. "We didn't do anything!"

My eyes trail toward the Gulf skies. Sun burns through the early morning rain, and blue shows between white fluffy clouds.

*The storm is coming. Isn't it?*

"This is foolishness," I tell Clay nervously, still studying the skies. "Why don't we hide a little longer, so when the storm comes—"

"Don't talk to me about that foolishness, Miss Witch," he growls.

Gisele rolls her eyes.

When we reach our homes, no police cars wait for us. I let out a breath I've been holding for several long moments.

Clay doesn't stop at my house and see me inside. He stomps right across our walkway and Gisele's to his own, climbs the steps in a hurry, shoves open his door, and slams it behind him.

Inside Gisele's house, something stirs at the noise. In a few seconds, Crazy Sardine swaggers out his door to meet us. He scoops Gisele into his arms. "Where you been? I looked all night."

"We hid from the fuzz, Daddy," she says. "And I'm gonna be a Amazon witch like Ruba, and I'm gonna help her beat up Za-Za's ghost who's out walking on waves."

Crazy Sardine gives her a smile as he puts her down. "Go on inside. Be there in a minute and make you some hotcakes." He kisses his daughter's head, and she skips up the stone steps and into her house.

Me, he regards with no expression at all.

"Sorry to worry you," I whisper. "When the police came—like Grandmother Jones said—we were afraid."

"I know. Maizie told me Leroy Frye's already making trouble, getting his friend to tell lies about some radio. She's worried about you, Ruba. Called here a bunch of times, and over to Hattie's, to see if y'all came in yet. I told her y'all were just hiding, but I think maybe you should use y'all's telephone first thing when you go in."

My toes are becoming a familiar sight to me. "I will. I didn't mean to make her unhappy."

As I turn away, Crazy Sardine heaves a sigh that could move leaves. "You make your grandmother happier than you know, you're so much like James Howard. But mercy, you look a lot like your mother, girl."

I turn back, curious. I know little of Circe, because it hurt Ba to speak of her. "Do I?"

"Yes. Like God took a picture, only turned it younger."

I smile where he can't see me.

"I remember her from Tougaloo, during the storms and all. I saw what she could do with weather and the wind. If you want to train Gisele like your mother and grandmother trained you, that's fine by me."

This time I look him straight in the eye.

Crazy Sardine shrugs. "Not everybody thinks magic is evil, especially not old magic. I think it's part of us, from way back. After Gisele's mother got killed in the march, I–I'm–well, I am what I am, and I'd be grateful for whatever you teach her."

I nod.

He nods.

"If you would let me train your daughter, you must trust me, Cousin."

"Yes, Ruba. I do. Just like I trusted Circe."

"If ever we find trouble together, will you do as I ask?"

He rubs the back of his neck and grins. "Probably will. Especially in a storm."

I cut my eyes to him, and he grins.

"Did you know my mother well?"

"Not very. She kept to herself at college. James Howard, he was smart like Circe. They made a good match. Both quiet, careful—but you could see the fight in their eyes. Feel their heart when they spoke, and my God, but they could give you that *look,* Ruba. That look says you're full of stuff and nothing, or that you just did the best thing in your whole life."

I think of Ba's eyes, of how I always knew her heart through her touch and words. And of Grandmother Jones and her rock face, and how when the warmth cracks through, I feel sun in my heart. I smile.

"Guess you got a piece of both of them," Crazy Sardine says. "Maizie Jones and Miss Ruba Cleo, too, though I never knew Circe's mother, rest them both. I see it when I look at you. When I listen. You're deep smart, like they were."

"Ba—um—Grandmother Ruba Cleo, she really did make me study. About Africa and history, the world, plants, the ocean—everything. And Grandmother Jones and Clay, they've been teaching me about the civil rights movement."

"I expect you're a fast learner, Ruba." Crazy Sardine shakes his head. "Gisele's a fast learner, too. She can keep up with you. I'm sure of it."

I shiver in my damp clothes, but somehow, I'm warm inside. Crazy Sardine gives me a wave and heads off to make Gisele's breakfast.

I find my own breakfast waiting on the stove. Biscuits still a bit warm in foil. Bacon and eggs. Juice already poured in a cup, just inside the refrigerator.

A note on the kitchen table instructs me to call when I get in, and I do.

"I was scared to death," is the first thing out of Grandmother Jones's mouth, followed by, "I never thought you'd stay gone all night. I ought to put you on restriction until next year!"

This is definitely not a time to make a stand—the pushing kind, the shoving kind, or any kind in between. "Yes, ma'am."

"And you know we can't be dodging Officer Bolin forever. We'll need to go down and talk with him, proper like. Tell the truth. I already called, told him we'd come by early in the morning tomorrow, before church."

I squeeze the hard plastic receiver, pressing it against

my ear. "Clay says we don't have a chance. Not if a white woman said we stole from her. Clay said we would go to jail."

"Maybe so, maybe not," Grandmother Jones says. "Clay Potts doesn't have the last say in things like that. But if you're going to live here and do a little pushing, you can't be scared of jail. Jail comes with the territory. If you get arrested, Hattie and I, we'll call the N-double-A-CP and get your bail, quick as we can." The National Association for the Advancement of Colored People. NAACP.

My breakfast looks less and less appealing. Jail worries me. Needing a group as powerful-sounding as the NAACP to get me out of jail scares me. Being in jail when Zashar's storm comes, that terrifies me.

"Ruba, I love you," Grandmother Jones says. "And I'll stand by you. This is little stuff, girl. I've seen a lot worse."

The emotional tone of her voice gets my attention almost as fast as her words. "I . . . love you, too," I say before hanging up.

My dress feels soggy and cold when I stretch it over a chair. I put on Grandmother Jones's dry robe. It smells of her, sweet and gentle, like rain on flowers. Not at all like Ba's strong scent of spice and smoke, but pleasant. Comforting. And I make myself eat, because it would please Grandmother Jones, and because I'll need my strength soon, for the storm chant.

Even with the scent of Grandmother Jones around me, I feel alone. And scared. The biscuits weigh heavy in my belly, and my feet feel like lead as I walk to my room.

It's a small space, but larger than what I had in Haiti. I kneel in the center and slide aside a small rug. There's a loose board, my one hiding place Grandmother Jones never finds. Other than my journal, my most important possessions lie underneath—my bow and quiver and the cowry shell necklace handed down through generations, that King Agaja's loyal son gave Tata in case we ever needed what strength of spirit the king had to offer. She wore it to remember King Agaja's son, her king, then gave it to her daughter. It came to me through Ba on the beach. I take it out with great care, and then retrieve the bow I so carefully repaired after Ba's death, the quiver, my sacred oils, and the Amazon war tunic Ba made me.

All seems in order.

Soon, I'll need these things with me. I'll need them close, for comfort and maybe even for safety. The most important thing before battle is to check your weapons, so I climb on the bed and do just that. First, I slide my machete out of my pillowcase, where it has lived since I came to Mississippi. I also fish out its leather strap, so I can polish the blade.

As I settle into my task, I hear an insane laugh far in the distance.

The unbalanced sound startles me into pausing, and I gaze out my window. The laugh comes again in its own time, unhurried.

It sounds mocking.

"Zashar has tortured another poor spirit and sent her out of the land of the dead," I whisper as I return to sharpening my machete. Only I know that laugh doesn't sound like any of the spirits I've heard before when Ba and I fought storms.

It sounds different, and completely without love or hope, and it makes me cold inside.

When I finish sharpening and polishing my machete, I check my arrows. They feel straight as I run my fingers from tip to end, and my bow—still true. When the time comes, I will retie its string and sling my quiver over my shoulder, and do what I must do.

Whatever that is.

If I'm not in jail for not stealing some white woman's radio.

I pack my secret things one at a time in a special bag, including the bow and quiver. I wrap a blanket around the bag and tuck it between my bed and the wall for hiding. Then I crawl under my covers to rest, just for minute.

The covers feel warm. My pillow, soft.

Grandmother Jones's robe hugs me as I sink into sleep.

. . . into wind, swirling . . .

. . . into skies, dark as a moonless night . . .

. . . into screams, raking the sea . . .

I jerk awake, heart pounding. It's still light outside. Did I sleep at all? And yet, the spirit in the storm on the ocean . . . she sounds so much louder.

And the smell of breakfast–a fresh breakfast, cooking–meets my nose.

*No!*

I leap from the bed and rush into the kitchen.

Grandmother Jones greets me with a smile.

"I didn't want to wake you," she says as I stand embarrassed and rumpled, still wearing her robe.

She doesn't mention it.

"Glad you slept the clock around," she says instead. "Needed your rest. Don't figure you've had such good sleep since you came to Pass Christian."

Good sleep. Full of nightmares and storms. I can't believe I dared close my eyes with a hurricane so near!

I can feel its breath on my flesh. Last night . . . last night. Light of the Creator . . . what I dreamed! That Zashar herself was in that storm.

That instead of fighting some tired spirit, some confused ghost needing to go back to the land of the dead–that I must fight Zashar herself. Here, now. When I don't even feel ready.

I dreamed that the stormwitch finally freed herself, that her spirit plows toward me, bent on death and complete destruction.

*Settle,* I instruct myself. *It was just a dream. Eat and speak to your grandmother and make her happy.*

Television news from a black-and-white set on the counter tells of nothing and more nothing. Grandmother Jones stands and parts the kitchen curtains with two fingers. Light spills across the table, across my dark, dark hands shaking as I hold a golden biscuit.

"You hear the television?" she asks.

I put down the biscuit and shade my eyes against the morning sun. "*Mais, non.* Um, no, ma'am."

"A big storm hit Cuba Friday night. Killed three people."

My hands shake so hard I have to put the biscuit down. My nightmares, barely held back, break on my mind like a storm surge. I try to manage my face, keep myself from leaping to my feet, grabbing my bag, and fleeing to the beach, where I feel I have some small power against the storm.

All that holds me in my chair is the belief that I will lose my grandmother's trust and respect if I go. And I can't leave her to face the police alone, or risk her being trapped in Pass Christian when the hurricane—and the spirit inside it—comes.

"They're calling it a hurricane now," Grandmother Jones says. "Hurricane Camille. And they say it might come this way. It'll probably dip under us and hit Texas like Betsy five years back."

My heart floods at the thought of Betsy, the name the whites gave the biggest storm I ever fought with Ba. It was my first real storm chant. In my mind's eye, Ba dances with her arms raised while I scatter spices on the beach.

Ba was still strong then. Her tall, lean frame moved like water itself.

It seemed so easy then. Scary and exciting, but somehow simple and . . . safe. Because Ba was there. Because Ba would make everything okay again.

I take a deep breath and let it out slowly, as I've heard Grandmother Jones do when she worries. "This Hurricane Camille," I tell her, "I think she will come here."

Grandmother Jones smiles. "You forecasting weather now?"

I study my toenails and nearby floorboards. "No. I mean, yes. I mean, well—Ba did. She taught me signs. Portents. Are those devil's work, too?"

"No, Ruba. Old folks have been reading the weather since before all memory. I don't put much stock in it, though. Now, go on and get dressed. We need to get to town."

"To the police. About that radio."

"Yes."

"What about Clay?"

"Clay is Hattie's problem for today, not mine. Though I expect they won't be far behind us. Probably just making some phone calls first. Hattie likes to have her support all lined up."

I wish I had my support all lined up.

As Grandmother Jones clears the table in her efficient, methodical way, I gaze at her small hands. They seem stiff and tense. She looks as stern as ever, but I don't feel so cold and alone. It's her warrior face, I remind myself. And women put on warrior faces when they want to protect what's theirs, when they don't want to lose something important.

*Then again, maybe I have all the support I need.*

As she finishes her cleaning, I slip into my room and take my journal from beneath my pillow and my bag from between the bed and the wall. I place the journal in the bag and hide it in a shadowed corner so I can reach it quickly. On my bed I spread my newest white cotton dresses, but they're dirty. And my African robes are still packed away. I stand in my underwear sifting through the frocks to find the one with the fewest stains, and I don't hear my door open until too late.

"My God in heaven, Ruba." Grandmother Jones

sounds shocked beyond measure.

I whirl around.

She points. "What is that blue horror on your belly and leg?"

I fumble to cover my crocodile, then slowly let my hands fall away. It's too large, and I know it.

Her eyes widen. She looks from the crocodile to my face.

"I—I'm an Amazon," I whisper. "Like I've told you. Or tried to tell you. This is the crocodile mark. This bracelet here, on my wrist. These are things Amazons wore before the French killed them all in Dahomey. Since Ba died . . . I'm the last."

Grandmother Jones has a stone face beyond all stone faces now. I see no anger in her eyes, but also no acceptance. No warmth. Something else. A flash and a flicker.

Fear?

Someone knocks on the front door, and we both startle.

I pull on a dirty dress and grab my bag as Grandmother Jones hurries out of my room, across the kitchen, and opens the door . . . to Officer Bolin.

"How do," she says, and drops her eyes to the floor.

"Maizie." He tips his hat to show the bristles of his close-cut hair.

I stand behind my bedroom door and seethe. *Mrs.*

*Jones,* I think. *Until you know her. Until you respect her and ask permission, her name is Mrs. Jones.*

"I found my granddaughter," she says. "I was just helping her get dressed before bringing her to you."

I clutch my bag and inch around the door, staring at the officer. The Man, Gisele calls him.

"Appreciate that, Maizie, but that's not why I'm here. They been flying recon out of Keesler Air Force Base in Biloxi, and those boys are worried about that storm. Hurricane Camille. I'm going door-to-door in the colored sections to let people know, seeing as lots of y'all don't have phones."

"Kind of you," Grandmother Jones says, and I hear the edge in her voice. "I do have a phone, in case you need to know."

The officer doesn't hear the slight edge of irritation in my grandmother's voice, but I do. He rubs the brim of his hat and keeps talking. "For now, I think y'all ought to leave. Go on inland."

Grandmother Jones raises her head. "I can't leave, Mr. Bolin. Over at the Richelieu, there'll be a hurricane party. I'll have to work."

Officer Bolin frowns. Seems ruffled. "Maizie, I got a bad feeling about this storm. Them idiots who want to watch the winds come, they're playing with fire this time. Please, take your granddaughter and go. I'll pay the apartments a visit and tell them I sent you away."

Grandmother Jones hesitates, then nods. "If you think it's best."

"I do." Officer Bolin turns his gaze on me. "And young lady, when this storm business is finished, you and I, we've got to have a talk about that radio."

"I didn't take any radio." I try to keep my eyes down, but I can't help looking him in the face.

He glares at me, and his cheeks color. "Maybe you did, maybe you didn't. We'll be talking."

Behind him, horns sound. Loud, like sirens, but low. Almost mournful.

"Civil Defense," Grandmother Jones says.

I'm still eye to eye with the policeman.

He looks away first.

Triumph makes me shiver. Push, not shove. Though this push may have some cost later, I don't care.

"Get going, Maizie," he says.

"Mrs. Jones," I say loudly.

"Ruba!" My grandmother's hand flies to her throat.

The officer's face goes slack. He looks both dumbfounded and perplexed, as if he has no idea what I mean.

"I'm from Haiti," I murmur, shifting my gaze to my hands. "In Haiti, it's polite to call older people by Mister or Misses. Is it so different here?"

Grandmother Jones is trying to speak, but her voice

seems to have failed her.

The officer still looks confused.

"This is my grandmother, sir," I tell him. "Even if you're angry with me, I hope you'll be polite to her, as I'd be polite to your grandmother. I'd call her Mrs. Bolin, not by her first name, like some little girl."

The officer coughs. "Yeah, well. Don't wait. Y'all get on out of here."

And he's gone, letting the door swing shut behind him.

Grandmother Jones wheels on me, eyes flashing. I swear her hair is sticking up. "Have you lost your mind?"

"No, ma'am," I say, then hold my breath, searching her face. Hoping.

She rolls her eyes.

And grins.

"Child . . . whooo." She fans herself with one hand. "I'm not believing–Hattie won't ever believe what you just did."

Her laughter fills the house, and I feel so happy I could cry. But I have no time to glory in the feeling. My grandmother is already rushing me.

"Come on, Ruba. Come on. We don't have time for this. Gotta find Sardis and Gisele and get out of here."

Sardis? Who is Sardis?

I would ask, but Grandmother Jones is dragging me out the door, bag and all. Down the steps, toward Crazy

Sardine's house. She leaves me on the porch and runs the poor man straight out of his bed. He has to beg her to give him time to put on clean pants and a shirt as he's hopping down the front steps.

Gisele, who has dressed faster in a blue smock and black shoes, holds my hand as I walk her to Grandmother Jones's yellow Mercury.

"We're going by the Richelieu first," Grandmother Jones says as she gets behind the wheel. Crazy Sardine gets in the front, while Gisele slides into the big backseat with me. "Then we're heading inland. Good Lord, the roads will be packed. I figure we should go on up to Tupelo, to my friend Netta's."

"Officer Bolin said he would speak to your boss for you," I remind her. All the while, I'm figuring how to get myself out of the car and have her take Crazy Sardine and Gisele on to Tupelo. To Netta's. Out of harm's way. That would be perfect. I'd be free to try my best to turn the storm, and the people I most care about, the family I have left, would be safe.

"I don't trust my job to anyone, child," Grandmother Jones says. "I'm going by there to tell them myself and get the time off."

"Ruba," whispers Gisele. "That witch in the wind, she's speaking foul. Somebody needs to wash her mouth out with soap."

"Yes, I know," I whisper back.

"Y'all hush," frets Grandmother Jones. "I'm trying to drive in traffic."

We inch onto the long coastal highway, joining what seems like every car along the Gulf. On my right, police lights swirl against a rising surf, and waves touch higher and higher on the sand. In the distance, rain falls over open water. On my left, trees and vines rustle and sway in the growing wind and gray light. Some people are boarding up their pretty mansions. Other mansions stand empty and dark with no cars in the drives. Owners at work, on vacation–or already gone, choosing safety over all else.

I look back toward the ocean, and a car on the road's shoulder with its hood propped open catches my eye. "Clay! Wait, Grandmother. There. Clay and Miss Hattie, broken down."

Grandmother Jones brakes.

Crazy Sardine hangs out of his window and motions for them.

Miss Hattie kicks one front tire on her blue car, and her lips move as she mutters all the way across the median.

Clay climbs into the front, and Miss Hattie squeezes in next to Gisele after I scoot over to give her some room. "Never buy another Ford," she swears. "Overheat if you look at 'em. Henry Ford must have made a bargain with the devil—and where you going anyhow, Maizie? It would be faster to head out the other way."

"They're throwing a hurricane party at the Richelieu, no doubt," Grandmother Jones says. "I'm supposed to work, so I need to tell them I can't come. I tried to call earlier, after I woke up, but I didn't get an answer."

"Hmmph," sniffs Miss Hattie. "They can damn well clean up their own mess this time. Bunch of fools."

"They've ridden out lots of hurricanes," Grandmother Jones says. "Won't be worried. The Richelieu's built solid."

"Hmmph," Miss Hattie grumbles again.

It's near noon by the time we make the three miles in traffic. The Richelieu Apartments stand proud against Camille's early kiss, and Grandmother Jones hurries out of the car, across a sidewalk, and through the main entrance, holding her plastic rain bonnet in place with one hand.

As I watch her disappear into the apartments, I know it's now or never. I have to get away to go fight the storm.

"Go on without me," I say where Gisele and Miss Hattie can hear. My hand closes over the cloth handles of my bag, and in one quick move, I open the door and start out of the car.

"Ruba!" Miss Hattie screams. She reaches for me as I swing the door shut.

My heart pounds as I run one step—and then rough arms catch me.

Not Miss Hattie's arms. One whiff of sweat and sour beer lets me know I've been caught by Leroy Frye.

Something sharp cuts into my throat.

# CHAPTER TWELVE

## Sunday, 17 August 1969: Afternoon

"Thought y'all might come here," Leroy Frye growls as he pulls me away from the car, keeping a knife tight against my throat. He heads us toward a small patch of woods that separate the apartments from other buildings. "Figured we could catch you before you left. Damn shame y'all are going to drown in the hurricane."

My elbow moves before my mind finishes a thought.

I connect with flab and bone and hear a great, "Uuunnnhh."

Leroy Frye's knife leaves my throat, and he lets me go. I stagger to the side, keep my balance, and keep a tight hold on my bag.

Miss Hattie huffs up beside us. "Serves you right," she spits at Frye, who retches on his knees and tries to breathe. "Worthless piece of–"

"Hattie!" Crazy Sardine appears at her side, holding Gisele, who is giggling. Clay runs up next to them, then stops and snickers. Over his shoulder, I can see the top floor of the Richelieu and the darkening sky.

"Well?" Miss Hattie uses her toe to nudge Frye, who's still on his knees, knife in hand, throwing up from where I planted my elbow in his gut. He manages to swing at her foot with his fist. "Asked for it, didn't you? Girl, you gotta teach me that move."

"Y'all think this is real funny, don't you?" someone calls from the nearby woods. A boy steps out and shakes his fist at us. I can tell from his square shape and what little I can see that it's Ray-boy's friend Poke.

"Coons with attitudes, all of 'em." This voice comes from my left, and it's Dave Allen.

"Guess we need to teach them some respect," says yet another voice from behind me, and this time, it's Ray-boy.

Cold metal presses against my ear.

*Click.* The sound snaps loud in my head.

"Good God," mumbles Miss Hattie. "The boy's got himself a gun."

"Come on now, nice and quiet. Back in the car," Ray-boy growls. "All of you."

Clay, Gisele, Crazy Sardine, Hattie, and I move back toward the Mercury, almost as one. My bag bumps against my leg, all the powerful things inside it useless because I can't get to them.

For now.

When we reach the car, Ray-boy shoves me around the still-open door and into the back seat. I drop my bag to the floorboard beneath my feet as he climbs in beside me. Poke and Dave Allen herd Miss Hattie and Clay into the front and Crazy Sardine and Gisele into the back next to me. They stand outside, though, not getting in, as if waiting for something.

To my horror, I see Grandmother Jones running toward us from the apartments, holding her keys. Her hand covers her mouth, and I know she has spotted the two boys standing outside our car. Maybe she can see Ray-boy in the back seat, too. And his pistol.

Leroy Frye stumbles up to the car then, clutching his belly as Grandmother Jones comes slowly around to the driver's side. He doesn't say anything, just grabs her and shoves her through the open driver's door, into the front seat. She settles behind the wheel, cringing, one hand up between her and Frye to protect her face.

"Move over," Frye orders her. "I'm driving. Boys, y'all follow. I'll go slow."

Gisele's eyes widen. She looks out her open door at Poke and Dave Allen, then slams it all of a sudden and punches the lock.

Ray-boy stiffens in the seat next to me.

Leroy Frye lowers his head to look into the car just as Grandmother Jones yanks the door, half hitting him, half knocking him sideways. He steps out of the door's path, and she slams it, locks it, and crams her keys into the ignition.

I slam my door and lock it faster than Frye can recover and get to it. He hammers on the window. Ray-boy shouts and waves his gun, but all the doors are shut and locked now. He's the only one inside with us. The rest are beating on the car for all they're worth.

The gun gleams as Ray-boy swings it back and forth through the air. Like some club, hitting nothing.

His father points at it.

Ray-boy doesn't see him.

The engine grinds and cranks.

Outside, Frye bellows and pounds and pounds on the car.

Grandmother Jones stomps the gas like she wants to stick her foot through the floor.

The car lurches.

Tires spin.

"Wait a minute," Ray-boy yells, only it's more like a scream. He's flapping his arms like a bird trying to fly, all the while whipping that gun back and forth. We all flinch as it passes us.

The car sails across the Richelieu grounds just as Ray-boy yells, "Stop!"

I see his hands go still. I see him grip the gun, touch the trigger.

Time seems to stop. My heart seems to catch like his

finger on that curved, deadly metal.

He fires the gun . . . and . . . and . . .

*Ba and I are dancing on the beach.*

*Time has no meaning.*

*Flower petals swirl in the waves.*

*Small waves.*

*The water is calm.*

*Ba looks at me.*

*She is frowning.*

*Pointing.*

*Pointing to the sky.*

"Open your eyes," someone is whispering. "Ruba! Dang it, open your eyes!"

I can barely hear over the ringing in my ears.

My face touches something cool.

Tile.

I try to move, but I can't. My hands are tied behind my back.

I manage to turn my head to the right.

I'm in someone's kitchen. A kitchen far bigger than the tiny space in Grandmother Jones's house. The floors are white tile with a green pattern in the center, and cold against my cheek. White counters shine under bright lights, and the stove seems new.

"Ruba," someone whispers. Hoarse and frightened. "Over here. This side."

I turn my head to the left.

Clay sits back to back with Gisele, bound to her with ripped towels.

Her head is down, chin against her chest, and her shoulders are shaking.

"You passed out because the gunshot was so loud in your ear," Clay says. "We're in somebody's mansion, right across the highway from the beach. Ray-boy made me break in through the boards on the back glass doors. Then he made me tie you and Crazy Sardine up with drapery cords. He and Mrs. Jones and Mama, they're behind you. Tied to some table legs. Ray-boy, he's gone to the toilet right now."

I immediately wish I could go to the toilet, too.

"Keep your head down," Gisele whimpers. "If he thinks you're making wind spells, he'll kill you. He said so."

"Mrs. Jones, she drove like a wild woman," Clay murmurs.

"I did not," Grandmother Jones whispers sharply from behind me. "You okay, Ruba?"

"Yes, ma'am," I say, as Clay keeps talking.

"She went busting through all that traffic. On and off the beach, in and out of parking lots, through yards—even one porch, until Ray-boy fired his pistol through the windshield. She liked to have wrecked us into an oak out behind this house."

"I did not," Grandmother Jones says again.

"Yes, you did," Miss Hattie grumbles. "Thanks to that half-wit white boy."

"Booger-head." Gisele draws a rattling breath and raises her chin a little. "He stuck his gun in my ear and I hit him. Lots of times, till he hit back and knocked me down. Then Daddy hit him, and he knocked Daddy out with the gun. Made Clay jimmy the back doors in this house, and then he brought us in here. Guess the owners already evacuated."

Footsteps thump in the hallway.

I turn my head away from Clay and Gisele and close my eyes halfway. Where it might look like I'm still unconscious.

Ray-boy slouches into the kitchen. He saunters to the giant green refrigerator and helps himself to cheese and beer and everything else he can grab. He carries the food to the nearest counter and plops it all down. Then he starts eating in a big hurry, nervous, almost like he's trying to make himself so full he can't be afraid.

As he stuffs food into his mouth, he watches us.

I watch him through my halfway-closed eyes.

"Go on," he says around a mouthful of hot dog. "Sit up, Juju Girl."

I open my eyes, but I can't sit up.

He swaggers over and jerks on my wrists. He pulls and

pulls. I cry out in pain despite my best effort not to, but manage to struggle up to a sitting position.

Ray-boy lets go of my wrists. He jams the gun into my head.

Cocks it.

I swallow hard. Gisele says something to herself, and I hear rustling. Probably Clay, fighting with his ropes. From behind me, Grandmother Jones prays.

Ray-boy moves the gun away and giggles.

I hear the hammer ease back into place.

Ray-boy walks back across the room to a telephone hanging on the wall beside the refrigerator. He puts the receiver to his ear and dials, his fingers making small circles and big ones. I hear the click of the dialing wheel as it rolls back into place between each number.

"Come on, Daddy," he says. "Answer so I can tell you where we are."

But apparently, no one picks up the telephone on the other end.

He hangs up.

A small television sits on a table across the room, near glass patio doors. Outside, trees dip and sway. The picture grows clear and goes fuzzy, a victim of the wind, but it speaks a clear message.

Hurricane Camille is moving toward us, covering fourteen miles every hour.

The news camera pans across people boarding windows and doors, or packing their belongings into vehicles. Lines of cars edge away from Pass Christian, Long Beach, Gulfport, Biloxi, Bay St. Louis, Pascagoula—from New Orleans to the Florida panhandle. People are fleeing north, waved on by policemen in rain gear.

Ray-boy studies the screen. "Damn idiots. I've been through two or three of these things. Hurricanes ain't nothing to worry about."

"Weatherman says it's a big one," Clay says in a low voice. "Winds over one hundred sixty miles an hour. We should leave."

"Yeah," Gisele says. "I heard him say there's waves twenty feet high."

"Shut up, pickaninny," Ray-boy snaps. He points his gun at Gisele.

She lowers her head.

Ray-boy laughs and turns back to the television.

I tug my knots with bent fingers until the knots come loose. I work them looser still, behind my back, and think of my bag in Grandmother Jones's car. I must reach it before the storm gets too far inland. If I can free one hand, get one second to myself, I can call the wind down on Ray-boy and get us out of this place.

Or get myself killed.

"You be still." Ray-boy bends to my face and presses

steel against my cheek. The gun barrel feels faintly warm, and I smell powder and fire.

"Listen to that news," I say. I keep my eyes straight ahead. My expression flat. "Hurricane Camille is coming. And they say she is worse than any before."

He grins, and his breath stinks of cheese. "Won't hit. They always say they'll hit, and they go to Texas. Daddy says the weatherman's stupid."

I think about arguing with him, but I tug against my bonds instead. Gisele jerks on hers, too, and so does Clay.

"Mighty big risk you're taking." Crazy Sardine's voice startles me. He stirs and groans.

"Daddy!" Gisele pulls against Clay.

"Shut up!" Ray-boy turns circles, swinging his gun up and down. Side to side. "Y'all be still and be quiet—that storm, it ain't coming here!"

He slams over to the phone and dials again.

"Sic the air on him, Ruba," hisses Gisele where only I can hear. "Quick, while he can't see."

"My hands are still tied," I tell her. "I've got to get them loose. If I chant, he'll hear me and shoot us all."

Grandmother Jones and Miss Hattie mutter to each other, but I can't hear them. Still, I think I know what they are saying.

They are asking God to keep Leroy Frye away from his telephone.

# CHAPTER THIRTEEN

## Sunday, 17 August 1969: night

By nightfall, Ray-boy is too nervous to be still. He lets us talk if we keep quiet about the storm, the gun, or getting away. Crazy Sardine, he's not saying much. Seems to drift in and out of knowing he's in a stranger's house with a hurricane coming.

To keep Gisele calm, I tell her stories about Africa and the Amazons.

"How big was Simpopi Palace?" she asks.

"Simboji. Huge. Bigger than you can imagine, almost four square miles."

"Mm-mm," says Miss Hattie. "Wouldn't want to be cleaning those floors."

"I hear that." Grandmother Jones laughs, and I smile.

"If you were a queen of Dahomey's Fon people," I tell them, "you would clean no floors. Every day you'd be rubbed in oils, and your hair would be styled, and you'd wear the finest, most beautiful cloth in all of Africa."

For a moment, I close my eyes, and I can almost see

Grandmother Jones in a dashiki. Then I come to my senses. "Fon kings lived in a splendor never seen in this country, Gisele."

"You mean you people have kings?" Ray-boy leans against a counter and chews on yet another cold hot dog.

"Great Negro kings," I tell him, pronouncing the word *neh-gro* the way I would say it in Haiti. "And each with a *kpojito* and many fine Amazons to guard him."

Ray-boy's shifty eyes narrow. He seems caught between disbelief and interest. "What's a po-whatever you said?"

"The Fon believed male and female had to be balanced, so every man in power had a woman to advise him."

"A woman could tell a man what to do in Africa?" Ray-boy laughs at this. "You gotta be kidding."

I shake my head. "No. I'm not. The king's mother-double, his adviser, could overrule him."

"Stupid country," he says. "No wonder we made y'all slaves."

"You made us slaves because you had guns, and you were greedy, and you could," Miss Hattie says with ice in her tone. "You needed strong backs to work cotton—white man's gold."

"Be quiet!" Ray-boy raises his gun and aims, and Miss Hattie falls silent.

"What are you going to do with us?" asks Grandmother Jones. "Are you aiming to kill two old women, three children, and a half-crazy man?"

I see the gun shake in Ray-boy's hand. He backs up against the far counter. For the smallest second, his eyes soften to a misty kind of scared, and he looks his age. Young-like and vulnerable. Then his expression freezes like cold water in winter, and he looks like a small version of his father again.

"Shut your mouth, you hear?" His voice is high, near to desperate. "Shut it and keep it shut."

We fall silent. I can sense the fine edge Ray-boy is walking in his mind, and I think the others can, too. Minutes creep by in the silence. The television picture has turned to static, and Ray-boy's father still does not answer his telephone. The sound of the storm—and the spirit in the storm—rises and falls. I try not to listen to it, but I can tell it's bothering Gisele, too.

When Crazy Sardine stirs again and wakes, I whisper his name and try to keep him awake and with us.

"Yes, Ruba," he mumbles. "My head hurts."

"One thing I have to know before this hurricane comes," I tell him. "Why do they call you Crazy Sardine?"

He snickers. "My momma did that to me. Named me Sardis, after that big lake upstate. All the kids at school called me Sardine."

"He got the *Crazy* part early in the Movement," Grandmother Jones adds. "When he ripped a water hose right out of a white man's hands during the Birmingham march."

"You marched in Birmingham?" Clay mutters. "I never knew that."

"The Man, he liked to turn these pressure hoses on us," says Crazy Sardine. "Those suckers burn and hurt. Feel like a hundred hands punching you all over. And I kept walking right up to this young deputy, and I took his away. Threw it on the ground, and it flopped till he ran off. But my wife got killed by a rock to the head a few marches later. Gisele, she was just a baby then."

Gisele sniffles.

"You shouldn't have been marching," snarls Ray-boy, back from the phone.

I stare at him, unable to hold back the rage in my eyes.

He blinks.

I see his gun droop, and I realize he was listening to us right along.

"Well," Miss Hattie mumbles. "Each entitled to their own thoughts, I suppose."

"We'll see," Ray-boy says. "We'll just see when my daddy gets here."

I close my eyes and work my knots. Sooner or later, this crazy white boy, he won't pay attention. Or he'll go to the bathroom again.

Sometime in the next hour, nature at last calls on Ray-boy Frye.

No sooner does he leave the room than I feel hands tugging at my bonds. A light scent. Rain on flowers.

Grandmother Jones. "Wait," she says. "Let me . . . there. There!"

I pull my arm loose.

Grandmother Jones heads for Gisele and Clay. I glance behind. Miss Hattie is helping Crazy Sardine.

I don't stop to think of consequences or plans. One purpose, and one purpose only. I must get my family and friends out of danger. Get them to the car.

And then get my bag and try to stop the worst of this storm.

We head out the jimmied back glass doors, into the soft rain, with me leading the way. Grandmother Jones, Gisele, and Clay are right behind me. Miss Hattie and Crazy Sardine bring up the rear, moving more slowly.

Down two steps.

Then three.

Onto the back stepping-stones, the grass.

Toward the car, which looks like it's joined to a large oak.

*The front is smashed. Will it start?*

My heart beats harder and harder. Footfalls and

muttering tell me the others are close behind me.

I throw open the back door and dive into the seat. My fingers close on my bag.

Grandmother Jones is getting behind the wheel. Clay and Gisele climb into the front seat beside her. I glance at the yard. Miss Hattie and Crazy Sardine are almost to the car.

"Why is it so dark?" Gisele whispers. "That big-mouth witch steal the moon and the stars, too?"

I glance toward the ocean and shiver, holding hard to the strap of my bag.

"Come on, come on!" Grandmother Jones cranks and cranks, but the engine refuses to catch.

"Marking Mercury off my list, too," Miss Hattie says loudly as she helps Crazy Sardine to the back door. "Stupid cars. Good Lord. Here comes that boy! Hurry, Maizie! Hurry!"

Ray-boy comes running from the house, gesturing with the pistol.

Crazy Sardine wobbles and staggers. He's trying to get into the backseat, but his balance is off.

"Stop it, y'all hear me?" Ray-boy yells through the rain and wind. "Get out of that car or I'll shoot!"

He points his gun toward Grandmother Jones.

I pull Gisele beneath me and duck. Try to pull Crazy Sardine inside the car.

"On the floor, Clay," Miss Hattie shouts, pushing him from the other side. "Get down!"

Grandmother Jones rolls down her window. "Put that gun away and come with us, child. Can't you see that hurricane's almost here?"

"Mm-hmm." Miss Hattie finally manages to get Crazy Sardine sitting down on the car seat. "You keep us here and we'll all be dying together."

"Nobody's going to die from this storm, you stupid coon." Ray-boy pushes Miss Hattie aside and stands in the open door, pointing his gun into the backseat—and Crazy Sardine half falls, half jumps out of the car and hits him square in the chest. The two of them tumble away from the car.

Ray-boy screams.

I struggle to get out of the car, then strain to see through the growing dark, through the growing rain . . . and a gunshot makes my ears go numb.

Gisele screams. And screams and screams.

I see two shadows roll away from each other. The shorter one gets up.

Ray-boy.

Crazy Sardine is still on the ground. Groaning. Holding his leg. Shot.

I shove Gisele back in the car and run toward him, carrying my bag. Wishing I could use it like a club, a club sharp with pasted shells and rock. A single blow to Ray-boy's thick head.

Rain hits me, harder now. Colder. I think about the pressure hoses at the marches Crazy Sardine talked about, and I refuse to slow down.

Ray-boy runs at me, crazy-like.

I drape my bag over my shoulder and raise my hands like I would to call the wind. He skids to a stop an arm's length in front of me.

"Ruba!" Grandmother Jones is yelling. "Ruba!"

Ray-boy aims his gun right at my head.

"P-put down your hands," he says.

For a moment, we just stand there, the boy with his gun and me with my hands in front of me like I'm going to hold him back.

And then I lunge forward and push him in the chest.

Ray-boy stumbles, but he doesn't fall. When he throws out his arms to gain his balance, I snatch his gun from his hand, raise it into the air, aim toward the boiling sky over the ocean, and fire it until it clicks and clicks and clicks. Then I throw it on the ground at Ray-boy's feet.

He looks up at me, shaking and surprised. I can tell he can't understand why I didn't kill him.

"Tonight, and only this night," I tell him, "and for my Grandmother Jones, I forgive you and I won't hurt you unless you make me. Now get over here and help us take my cousin inside."

Ray-boy makes no effort to move. He narrows his eyes. They dart back and forth like he's trying to choose some other option. He chews his lip.

Miss Hattie and Grandmother Jones arrive in time to give him two small pushes of their own.

Not shoves. Just pushes.

He stumbles forward, toward the house.

"Go on, child," Grandmother Jones says to Ray-boy in a voice like iron. "Help Sardis. If you're big enough to make a mess, you're big enough to help clean it up."

Behind her, Clay fights to hold Gisele back. She's flailing like she wants to murder Ray-boy and leave his bones for the crows.

I take her from Clay's arms, dodging her blows as she screams, "Daddy! I want my daddy! Why did you hurt my daddy, you ole cracker booger-head? Why? I hope the storm kills your daddy! I hope you have to know how bad it feels!"

Ray-boy stands still. He gazes at Gisele as if seeing her for the first time. Then his head droops, and he stares at his feet. Moving slower than slow, he bends down, picks up the useless gun, and puts it in his waistband. With a final, baleful glance at Gisele and then the storm, he seems to sag, to bend like a little tree in the wind.

Does he understand what's real now?

That the storm's here, and he can't do a thing to stop it, no matter the color of his skin?

Maybe.

Maybe not.

Whatever he's feeling behind those narrowed, darting eyes, he helps Clay and Miss Hattie drag Crazy Sardine back into the house. I carry my bag and Gisele, who wails for her father almost as loud as the winds wails at the trees.

Inside, I hand Gisele to Grandmother Jones, and Miss Hattie helps me find my cousin's wound—in the left thigh. It looks like a giant cut instead of the hole I expected, and it's deep. We bind it above and below with the same ropes we only just escaped, and I use a few of the herbs from my bag to slow the bleeding. Then I cover it with cloth strips from the towels Ray-boy tore to tie up Clay and Gisele when we first got here.

Ray-boy stands pale and shaking in the kitchen as gusts of wind rattle windows despite the hastily placed boards. Somewhere in the distance, bigger winds howl. We hear low moans, like the sound of a haunting. Like the sound of death risen to speak.

"We've got to get him to a hospital," Clay says as I once more press a bloody towel to Crazy Sardine's leg.

"Can't," Grandmother Jones says, only she is yelling to outdo the wind. "Never make it in this weather. Besides, they'll be evacuated by now."

"What about the air force base?" asks Ray-boy.

I swallow my shock at the fact that he offered a suggestion.

"Too far." My grandmother rubs her chin.

"We could hide in the basement," Gisele says.

"No." Miss Hattie shakes her head. "There'll be heavy surf coming in before winds that strong. We could drown down there."

"Upstairs," I say. "High ground is safer than low, and we can use mattresses to cover ourselves. I've been through many storms like this in Haiti."

All eyes fall on me, and Grandmother Jones frowns. I clench my teeth and study her.

"So be it," she says at last.

It's nearly ten o'clock by the time Clay and Ray-boy manage to drag Crazy Sardine up the shiny wooden steps to the second floor of this mansion owned by strangers who are, I hope, safe from the storm.

Safer than those of us left behind in their house, at least.

Grandmother Jones finds the biggest bedroom, and Miss Hattie and I pull all the mattresses to that spot toward the back of the house. We have three big mattresses in all, and three box springs. I lash the box springs together by the handles with tight ropes until they look like a strange gray barge. Fragile. Good for minutes, or maybe an hour.

"These won't hold long if we have to float," Miss Hattie observes, tugging plastic and fabric.

"Maybe long enough," says Grandmother Jones.

We tie Crazy Sardine onto one of the box springs and cover him and Gisele with a mattress. They lie sandwiched between the fabric, tied tight, but loose enough to still breathe. I can see Gisele's bright eyes through the shadows between the box spring and the mattress. They follow me as I move, left and right. Back and forth.

Clay and I pile onto the next box spring while Ray-boy stands to the side, head down.

Finally, Grandmother Jones gives him a little tap on the shoulder. "Go on. Lie down. I can't cover you up if you keep standing there."

This seems to surprise Ray-boy so much he can't say anything. He hesitates, glancing at the mattress. The winds give another huge howl, and that helps him decide. He crawls on beside me, and Grandmother Jones covers us with a mattress and gives us blankets to shield our heads if we need them when the time comes. The wind drives the rain hard enough to feel like nails, and anything flying around will stick straight through us if we don't have enough padding. I grip one side of the fabric and hug my bag to my chest. Thanks to Ray-boy and all he's done, I'll have to wait until the eye comes now, until the spirit's all the way here.

It'll be a harder fight, and dangerous. Fighting the storm in the eye got Ba killed. The winds can shift so fast. . . .

Grandmother Jones and Miss Hattie open the windows as my ears begin to hurt. My skin aches along with my belly. Those unboarded upper windows don't stand a chance against the pressure of the storm.

"Whatever debris comes through," Hattie says, "I figure that'll be better than flying glass."

They lie down on the last box spring, as if to sleep, and pull a mattress over them.

"Ray-boy," I hiss through my teeth. "This storm isn't natural. You might not believe me, but you're going to see bad things. Awful things. No matter what, don't speak to any figure that comes. Let me handle it. I can stop it if you'll stay out of things."

"What you talking about?" He stares at me in the semidarkness, his face oddly mashed by the mattress. His hair hangs limp near his nose, and he struggles to get his arm up and wipe it out of his eyes with one hand.

"Remember what happened in the woods? At the church?" I gaze at him without blinking. "You were right. I'm a juju girl."

He smiles with half a mouth. Nervous. "Don't be trying to scare me, girl."

"My name is Ruba, and I can save you from what's coming. It's up to you."

"I ain't trustin' no—" Ray-boy starts.

"Coon," I growl. "Jigaboo, darkie, pickaninny—whatever you want to call me. You think those names make me less than you? You think calling people names makes you strong? Well, go on, strong man. Get out there and stop this storm."

"You're crazy," he says.

"She is," Clay agrees from Ray-boy's other side. "But her name is Ruba. Say it."

Ray-boy turns his head to glare at Clay, then back at me.

"Say it." I stare right back at him, refusing to lower my eyes. "Then don't say another word till this is over, if you want to live."

Ray-boy's mouth opens. His face turns purple-red. I brace myself for the swearing. The insults. The words of hate and loathing I know live within him.

"Ruba," he grunts, and turns his head away from me.

We lie without moving as the storm and its spirit finds the coast.

Lights flicker and go dark.

Around half past ten, shrouded by the unforgiving

Mississippi night, Hurricane Camille slams ashore in Pass Christian.

The wind roars like a monster from time before time.

Around us, the mansion rattles and shakes, a dollhouse in Camille's cruel hands. Branches and bricks and dark shapes thunder against the house while trees crack and split to toothpicks. A branch crashes through the roof near where we're huddled, and rain pelts the walls.

I clench my bag to my chest and hold my breath. The roar in my ears feels almost unbearable, but if I start my chant too soon, I might get knocked down or drowned, and all will be lost. Now that the beginning's past, I have to wait for the eye.

Through the wicked gales I hear a more sinister noise. A slapping, a gentle slapping, steady and sly.

"What is that?" Clay hollers in my ear.

"Waves!" I holler back.

I see the horror in his eyes as the truth swallows him. The Gulf of Mexico has broken her bounds, and she's knocking on our door. The ocean has surrounded the house.

Seconds whirl by. Minutes. Windows shatter. Through the unceasing scream of the storm, I hear water pouring into the house. Flashes of lightning show me torrents of rain through the open windows from my vantage point between the mattress and box spring, slamming toward earth but never reaching it, swept back up in the wind. A small space exists between rain and water, an impossible space, made by sheer force and danger.

I can hear an upstairs wall ripping away, and immediately my hair is nearly pulled from my head. The wind sucks at us so hard the mattresses start to move.

Around me, mouths are open, yelling, but I hear only the wind. I chew my lip and my exposed side stings from rain. My teeth chatter.

Another chunk of the house blows loose, and the structure rocks sideways, dipping like a carnival ride.

At that moment, I hear drums, and above those, a round of horrible, unnatural swearing.

The spirit in the storm, the evil. It's here.

It's time for me to fight.

I battle the mattress to loop my bag about my neck, scoot out from under the protection of the fabric, and force myself to my feet in the now-unsteady mansion. No one sees me because they have their heads covered, sandwiched between the mattresses and box springs.

It takes all my strength to stand, and more strength than I believe I possess, to raise my arms above my head.

I start the chant.

"Circe and Ruba Cleo, I call on you, my foremothers. Protect me. Antoinette and Arielle, give me the strength of our people before white men and guns and steel . . ."

The song floats soundlessly against howling gusts as my fingers reach and my hands turn in circles, working the spell. From my bag, I add spices to the wind, and I turn my hands some more as I chant.

Time seems to spin to a stop between my palms, but my muscles tighten from the pressure. I feel like I can barely move.

How can I do this on my own?

The wind howls on, heedless of me and my efforts. I can't hold the spell. It breaks as my hands drop and my arms fall to my sides.

But I keep chanting.

I chant the names of my foremothers until my jaw locks and I try to lift my hands again, to tame the winds. To stop them, at least in the space where I'm standing, and where my family and friends and Ray-boy huddle between the mattresses and box springs.

Nothing happens. It isn't working!

*My family . . . my family . . .*

A flash of white catches my eye, and I stare at it as I finally manage to raise my arms over my head. Teeth . . . a smile.

For a moment, I fall silent.

Gisele. Peering at me from under her mattress. She is smiling.

I smile back and pry open my unwilling mouth, and I

start the chant over again.

"Circe and Ruba Cleo, I call on you, my foremothers. Protect me. Antoinette and Arielle, give me the strength of our people before white men and guns and steel . . ."

I turn my hands in slow circles again, and a glow flickers in my fingers. A circle. A small bubble. It swells and grows, expanding to cover me, and then most of the room, from the floor to a few feet above my head.

Soon, I stand in light and silence. The bubble spreads a little farther, first left and then right. Up and then down. All around the room it travels, blocking out the storm until the only sound is my voice raising the chant.

"Is it over?" Crazy Sardine mutters.

"No, Daddy," says Gisele. "Ruba's sending the wind away."

"My God, Maizie!" Miss Hattie's voice trembles. "What's she doing?"

Grandmother Jones doesn't answer.

I know she might not forgive this. My conjuring might split us down the middle. The juju. The old magic of Dahomey's Fon, the proud Amazons. But if she's alive to throw me from her home, so much the better.

Clay and Ray-boy lie behind me, motionless under their mattress, caught in the web of my spell.

My bubble closes and gains its full strength, and not a moment too soon.

I see the walls of the mansion shake, then watch as the great house starts to move beneath us. The bubble keeps us still, keeps us protected, but my senses feel the shuddering, hear the splinter of wood and crack of stone as the mansion loses its battle with the wind and the wild, angry ocean.

In moments, the big house washes completely off its foundation. It sweeps out from under us, falling into heaps of boards and debris, captured in the waves—but we stay suspended in the air. We float easily in the bubble I made, hovering above the spot where the house once stood. We barely bob at all, despite the water and the wind.

So far, my magic is holding. One slip of concentration, one moment of doubt . . . I push away such thoughts. Keeping one hand raised toward the stars, I use the other to twist my bag off my neck and open it.

"Help me," I say to Gisele, and she wriggles from beneath her mattress.

She nods.

With her assistance, I keep my hand raised but manage to strip off my cotton dress, and once more I hear Miss Hattie. "Would you look at that tattoo? I've never seen anything like that. Covers half her leg—all the way to her waist! It's a blue alligator."

"Crocodile," says Gisele, and she helps me into my war

tunic. Shells and bones clatter against my skin, Amazon armor like my foremothers wore. "And don't talk to nobody but Ruba. Nothing, nobody, okay, Miss Hattie?"

I hear Grandmother Jones begin to pray.

"Can Mrs. Jones and Miss Hattie talk to God, Ruba?" Gisele asks as she fastens the tunic. "Would that be okay?"

I nod. "Just don't talk to anything in the storm. Everyone will have to trust me for that."

The drums grow louder.

"She's coming, isn't she?" Gisele shivers as she loops the last shell-anchored tie. "It's not a ghost this time, like you've fought before. It's that witch you talked about. The one who wants to kill you."

"Yes," I tell her, feeling tightness in my throat, my chest. "I'm afraid Zashar herself is in the storm. Just a few steps away from us."

*17 August 1969*

*Dearest Ba,*

*It seems only right to talk to you now. If I dared to pull out my journal, I'd write this down. Somehow, I think you'll be able to hear me, though. Even if I'm speaking only in my mind.*

*I'm standing before the eye of the storm. It's almost here.*

*I'm wearing my war tunic of bones and shells. My body is drenched with palm oil, and I'm girded with my war belt. My machete hangs at my waist, and my bow and quiver are slung over my shoulder.*

*Gisele has placed my white cap on my head.*

*As befits a palace guard, an elite protector of Dahomey's finest king, I now stand fully dressed for battle. The blue crocodile slides up my leg and sits above my brow, as if sewn on my cap, waiting.*

*My hands make fists. One raised. One by my side. King Agaja's necklace lies at my feet, in case I need his memory to keep my courage.*

*I'm an Amazon. I've come to fight this storm.*

*My hands will be steady this time. I won't wait too long to shoot.*

*I'm ready for Zashar—and it's at this moment that I think of you—and I falter.*

*My mind climbs backward in time to our last storm together.*

*I see you standing next to me on Haiti's sand as the little hurricane swirled toward the shore.*

"Il n'est pas Zashar," *you whisper as the wind twists toward us. "Next time, it might be her, and we could end this forever. We're the last, child. And the last will have to do what all the rest couldn't, or things will go bad for this world."*

*Even now, I still feel your warm, oiled fingers in mine. I see the crinkle of your eyes when you smile, Ba. And then Agontime's unexpected turn . . . the tug . . . her shouting . . . your smile . . . your hand, leaving mine.*

*And I remember.*

*You were smiling as you started to go under because of what Agontime was saying. About enough, about finishing this fight.*

*And you said, "This is right. Believe it's right. Sometimes you have to let go to hold on."*

# CHAPTER FOURTEEN

## no time, no Place

We're all on our feet now, except Crazy Sardine. He's awake, and he throws off his mattress before pushing himself to one elbow.

"Are we flying in the air?" Miss Hattie asks from behind me.

"Yeah." Gisele turns to face her as I keep my eyes forward, on the walls of rain that mark the storm. "Looks like a soap bubble, doesn't it? Ruba sent the wind away and put us in the soap bubble."

"I don't think the wind's gone," says Grandmother Jones, pointing to bending trees all around our small, bright bubble. We can see only the top halves. "It's still blowing."

"We're sailing," I whisper. "Sailing on the storm."

"I'm dreaming," chants Clay. "I'm dreaming, I'm dreaming. . . ."

The first footfall shakes the universe.

We sway inside the bubble.

"What in God's name was that?" Miss Hattie shouts.

"That's got nothing to do with God," says Grandmother Jones.

"The stormwitch is coming," I tell them. I wheel around and glance into each pair of wide eyes. "No matter what you see, believe. No matter what you hear, don't respond to it. Don't speak to anything in the storm. No matter how well or poorly the battle goes, trust me, and you might live."

All nod—except Grandmother Jones.

Another footfall slams against the coast.

Grandmother Jones sets her mouth in a straight line, and her face holds stark anger. "You brought this on us," she says in a cold voice.

"This vengeance is far older than me," I tell her. "Please, just don't speak to her."

Grandmother Jones does not believe me. I can see it in the tilt of her chin. "Admit it, Ruba. You put some spirit in this storm."

"It's the stormwitch, Grandmother, like I've been telling you."

"Foolishness."

*BOOM!*

"What is that?" bleats Clay. "You're nuts, Ruba!"

Ray-boy kicks the mattress now lying beside the box spring. He's holding his breath, nearly blue in the face, so badly does he want to speak.

I glower at him. "This is partly your fault. You stopped me from chanting the storm while it was weaker, still at sea. I could have taken on the witch better then, but now—this is what I have to do."

Another thundering footstep makes my bones ache. "You just pray to whatever you believe in. Pray I can send Zashar back to the land of the dead."

"And if you don't?" Clay asks.

"She'll kill us." I shudder. "Then she'll keep walking, and take this storm inland. She'll cover the whole world in her hurricane, for as long as she can. She's evil and angry, and she'll hurt as many people as possible."

My eyes return to Grandmother Jones. She says nothing.

"I fight on the side of right," I whisper.

"Not my right," she murmurs. "My god is the only right way."

"Then speak to him!" I yell. "I'm not stopping you. Your god is mine, and mine, yours."

Miss Hattie touches Grandmother Jones's arm just as the world grows still and yet another footfall shatters our peace.

"The eye's here," I shout, too nervous to keep my voice low.

A laugh drifts forward, high and wild, like the mad

yelp of a starving dog.

A cold light fills the stillness of the bubble I created. The moon and the stars break through drifting clouds. A shadow falls across me.

Gisele screams.

Miss Hattie gasps.

Grandmother Jones lifts her prayers toward heaven, and Ray-boy Frye starts to cry.

From Clay and Crazy Sardine, there is but a stunned silence.

I straighten my shoulders and try to stand tall. "Zashar," I say.

"A child?" screams a voice straight from the depths. "Agaja sends a child against me? I did not think to have it so easy. Where's the old one? Where is Ruba Cleo?"

I lower my raised fist, drop my hand behind my head, and withdraw an arrow from my quiver. My bow slides from my shoulder into my palm.

"She's gone. I'm the only Amazon left for you to kill . . . if you can."

I see her then.

Six sharp gasps tell me that the others see her, too.

Zashar towers as large as a mountain, dressed just as I am, wearing a guard cap so white it lights the night. Her crocodile mark winds dark blue and harsh against her ebony skin, and her crusted teeth seem sharp and brutal.

Bones rattle on her tunic. Moonlight flashes on her machete. A rifle as large and long as any cannon hangs in her belt. The stock droops heavy with cowry shells pasted in place with blood, one mollusk for each soul she has killed in battle.

Her right hand is raised, and her left is closed at her side.

*Is she holding more shells? One for me, one for each of the people I love?*

"Stand aside," she rumbles.

I shake my head and nock the arrow. "No."

She laughs and waves a hand. A great gust topples me backward. Beside me, Ray-boy covers his ears, and Clay shakes.

I struggle back to my feet, grateful I didn't lose my bow or the arrow.

"Who are these?" Zashar snorts. "Old women, weak men—and a white beast? Give him to me. I'll eat him first. If you give him to me, I'll spare one of the others. One of the old ones, if you ask it. Give him to me!"

Ray-boy cowers closer to Clay, and Clay actually throws a protective arm across his shoulders. I can tell with one glance that Ray-boy is sure I'll do this, that I'll sacrifice him to save my grandmother.

The thought does tempt me, but only for a second.

"You'll go hungry," I say. "He's under my protection,

just like the rest."

"Your protection?" The witch rattles the bubble and knocks me down again, this time harder. My face scrubs against the edge of a box spring and I feel my cheek bleed. "You make me laugh, girl."

Once more, I find my feet and resettle my bow and arrow.

Zashar leans her hard black face into the bubble, toward Gisele, who stands silently at my side. "And you, little mouse. Come here. Let me see you."

Gisele holds her ground. Brighter light swells around her, and Zashar steps back. "What is your name, little mouse?" she booms.

Gisele opens her mouth. My heart stops, but I can't interfere with the choices of others. If she speaks to the witch, Zashar might confuse her and claim her.

I watch, chewing my own tongue, as Gisele slowly closes her lips. She glances at me, and she turns her back on the witch.

Zashar's attention strays to Crazy Sardine. "You there, on your backside. Who might you be?"

Crazy Sardine gives me the same glance as his daughter, lowers himself back to the box spring, and closes his eyes.

Clay and Miss Hattie don't wait to be addressed. They turn from the witch before she calls them out.

"White boy!" shouts Zashar. "Have you come to speak for your own?"

Ray-boy flushes scarlet, but he doesn't answer.

"Worse than grub worms, the white lot," the witch continues. "Fat and pale, sloppy and sticky. You take what you can get."

Ray-boy's fists open and close, but he looks at me. I stare back without moving. It's his choice.

Purple and sweating, he crams one fist in his mouth and flips over on the mattress.

And then Zashar's chilly gaze passes to Grandmother Jones.

"I hear you speaking to your white god," says the witch, and I worry. Grandmother Jones insists her god has no color, and she feels strongly about that.

Will she start an argument with the witch?

"You fancy this god a match for me?" Zashar asks.

Grandmother Jones trembles.

"Call him, then, old woman! Call down your god, or deny him with your silence!"

Grandmother Jones steps forward. She stands at my shoulder and stares at Zashar's dark, foul bulk.

Outside our bubble, the trees begin to move again, ever so slightly, ever so gently, and I know the moment is coming.

I make myself keep my eyes on the witch and away

from Grandmother Jones. If I look at my grandmother, I'll beg her to be silent. I'll sob and tell her how I don't want to lose her, too.

I feel the soft brush of Grandmother Jones's lips against my cheek.

"My god taught me not to talk to the devil," she whispers in my ear, speaking to me and not the witch. "My god taught me not to give the devil any openings at all. That's why you want us to be quiet. I understand."

Then, I hear a rustle as she drops stiffly to her knees without comment to Zashar. She folds her work-worn hands, and closes her eyes. Speak she does, but in her own mind, to her own god and not to the witch.

"You stand alone, girl," Zashar says to me.

"No," I tell her. "You do." I thrust out my bow. The arrow rests lightly against my finger. With my toe, I kick Agaja's necklace, and I fire the first shot. It slips through our floating bubble, leaving a ripple in its wake.

Smoke and shimmers billow forth from the necklace, catching Zashar's eye as my arrow flies true. She doesn't notice it to dodge. While she stares at the necklace, the arrow strikes her large left knee. She still doesn't seem to be aware of it.

"Aaahhh," she hisses as the smoke from the necklace takes form around me.

A shadow-man stands with me now, handsome and

youthful. His robes twinkle, brilliant silk, and he wears heavy pearls and glittering hammered gold.

"Begone, witch," says Agaja, and he waves his beautiful wispy hands.

I fire my second arrow into Zashar's right knee. Another ripple in the bubble, another true hit. She feels this one, and the other, and to my surprise, she sinks like Grandmother Jones in prayer.

"Once I killed your memory," she growls to Agaja. "I killed your sons. It pleases me to kill your spirit, fool!"

She reaches for him, her hand pushing farther and farther into the bubble. The bubble shifts and distorts. It trembles, as if it might burst. My third and final arrow trembles against my finger, too. My nerves jangle. My arrow dips.

Zashar's hand nears the spirit of King Agaja.

Suddenly, behind the witch's head, I see a new glow. First one, then two, then flare after flare after flare. A face!

Ba's face, grinning broadly.

And then another face, much like Ba's. It must be Circe, my mother.

The witch's hand falters and slows.

One by one, the stars come to be counted. Amazons beam at me from the sky, the white of their guard caps shining.

I straighten, and my arms feel young and strong. I gaze into the loving faces of my Amazon ancestors.

"Go back to the dead," I yell at the witch, and I let fly the third arrow.

It leaves a bigger ripple in the bubble, then sails forward, a dream shaft, and lands between two strands of Zashar's tunic. Just a prick to the heart, small as a pin, but tipped with love and the strength of all the generations of Amazons.

Zashar's hand stops inches from the neck of my king, but still, she doesn't fall, and she doesn't retreat. I can tell she's weakened, but not defeated.

The bubble holds against her thrust, but for how long? My body starts to shake.

I've fought her in all the ways Ba taught me. She's half broken, and yet she stays. What's left to do? I glance desperately at my bag. My herb jars have been broken and scattered. My oils are spilled. My machete is gone. There aren't any extra arrows. My journal is the only thing left.

Shrugging off my quiver and dropping my bow, I reach for it. I don't know what else to do.

Zashar, her hand still inches from Agaja's spirit, watches me with mean, gleeful eyes.

I snatch up the journal and wield it like a shield.

And then, thinking of Grandmother Jones and all

she's taught me so far, I take the journal, step forward, and say, "Go. You won't win. Together, we're too strong for you."

Holding the journal with both hands, I use the book to give Zashar's outstretched hand a gentle push away from us.

To my surprise, the witch screams as I make contact. Where I touched her bubble-coated fingers, the walls of the magical shield harden and reject her.

She stands, then staggers and throws back her head.

"Aaaahhhh!" she bellows, holding the hand I touched with the journal, giving off blasts of wind strong enough to fell buildings and mighty oaks. They penetrate the bubble like my arrows, rippling, but leaving it intact.

I hold up my journal and chant, using the book to knock away the gusts. They spin back outside the shield I made.

"Aaaaahhhh!" Zashar shrieks, and the wind around our bubble grows steady. It buffets the rounded shield, tossing it like a child might toss a marble, up and down. Back and forth.

Grandmother Jones topples over, but I hold the journal in one hand and grasp my grandmother's hand with the other. Miss Hattie joins the chain, and Clay, and Crazy Sardine. Ray-boy pushes in between them.

The bubble starts to dissolve. Wind breaks in. We are

whipped around like feathers, anchored only by my grip and my will. Beneath my arm, Gisele somehow stands, and I see her reach toward my upraised arm.

*Hold on to them,* Ba seems to whisper in my ears. *It's not your time to go. You have years of love and battles ahead.*

My legs grow weak.

Zashar thrashes.

The bubble sinks, lower and lower, losing its shape steadily as it plunges us into the wild surf.

Wind and water slam against me, an elephant made of storming air and waves.

I stand, and I stand, on the bit of protective bubble still holding us up. Then, I feel Gisele's fingers close over my elbow. She clings to me and I cling to her as Zashar's winds turn on her. The witch strikes out at the swirling storm, but it strikes back. It seems to have teeth. A mouth. Opening wide, wide, wider to swallow her.

The sea itself snaps at her, each bite making her less and less whole. Less and less real. Less and less here, less and less now.

Zashar runs away, kicking tides and waves as she goes. Back into the ocean, the darkness. Back into death.

She doesn't look back.

The bubble sags.

We fall into the ocean, but I feel no pain, no cold, no fear. Light blinds me, and . . .

*I see you, Ba, holding the gates between life and death, ready to close them behind Zashar.*

*You're standing with my mother, waving. You look like you did when I was little, strong and full of energy. I see you blowing me kisses while King Agaja fades back into memory, and Zashar's winds pound her farther and farther into death, where she can never find her way back.*

*And if she does, you'll be there. With my mother. With my foremothers. Guarding the gate.*

*I feel Gisele's hand on my arm. I feel Grandmother Jones squeeze my fingers in hers, and I know. The Amazons live, Ba. In us. In me. In my family.*

*This is my first victory.*

*On the beach in Haiti—I think I understand.*

*I didn't fail you. I didn't let you go.*

*It was you. You let go of me, because you were sick and your strength was failing. You knew Zashar was coming because Agontime told you, and you trusted me to be strong enough to defeat her. You let go so that in the end, we could hold on.*

*I will always love you, Ba. I will always sense you in the night stars. My father, my mother, my grandmother, gone before me, but I'm not alone. I'm far from alone now.*

*Good-bye, Grand-mère Ruba.*

# CHAPTER FIFTEEN

## Sometime, Someplace: After

A gentle rocking wakes me.

I'm floating, holding my wet journal to my chest with both hands.

Salt water laps my face. Rain drizzles across my body. My head rests on soggy cloth. I feel my tunic against my aching skin, wet with seawater and stained with my blood.

I sit up on a mattress in the ocean.

No! Not the ocean.

I'm bumping against a toppled cornice. Tops of trees poke through waves around me.

The ocean has swallowed Pass Christian, Mississippi.

I sink back to the waterlogged cloth and see nothing.

# CHAPTER SIXTEEN

## Monday, 18 August 1969

"Ruba?"

Someone shakes my shoulder.

"Ruba, open those eyes!"

My body feels still, though my mind has that floating sensation. I feel wet mattress with one hand and wet, hard ground with the other. The air smells wet and dank and dirty. I force my eyelids to cooperate, and Miss Hattie's worried face blurs into view.

"Storm over?" I rasp, getting to my feet in sand and muck. My mattress apparently beached itself on branches and debris, and held fast as the storm surge pushed back out to sea.

"In a manner of speaking," Miss Hattie says. She wraps the shreds of my cotton dress around me, covering my tunic.

Clay's face looms at her elbow.

I step off my mattress, hearing it squish beneath me. Miss Hattie helps me keep my balance and not drop my journal.

The other things I lost, my bow and quiver, Agaja's necklace—my mind soothes me by reminding me of Ba's words in my ears. I held on because it wasn't my time. Those things from my past, they're gone because maybe it *was* their time to be lost.

My family doesn't need them anymore. The storm-witch is back in the land of the dead, maybe for good.

"Good Lord, girl." Miss Hattie pats my head. "I thought you washed away with that house. With all the houses."

I glance left and right. Behind Miss Hattie and Clay lies what is left of Pass Christian, Mississippi—and that's nearly nothing at all.

Seawater makes pools and ripples, and a light rain falls. Buildings are nothing but boards. Cars sit in boats that perch on heaps that might have been houses. Sand lies in piles like small mountains, and only a few trees stand.

"Where is everybody else?" I wheeze, shivering at masses of snakes writhing on all available flat surfaces.

"We're all here, child," says Grandmother Jones. I feel her arm drape my shoulder, and I bury my face in her wet dress. "Dang snakes. Looks like Satan's kicked them all out of hell's bayous. They're everywhere!"

When I turn my head, I see ambulance drivers working on Crazy Sardine. One stands long enough to kick a snake into a puddle. It flops and wriggles away.

"On my count," says the other ambulance man. "Three, two, one," and the men lift my cousin into an ambulance.

"Where are they taking Daddy?" asks Gisele in a tiny voice as the truck lumbers away through debris.

"To a hospital tent," says Officer Bolin. I see him standing with a hand on Ray-boy's shoulder.

To my horror, Leroy Frye stands next to his son. His arms are folded, and his eyes speak the hatred he feels.

"The radio," I whisper.

"I'm not here for a radio, girl," Officer Bolin says. "That man Sardis was shot, and I need to know how it happened."

I scratch my shoulder, and my nails slide on the remnants of palm oil. My eyes flick to Ray-boy, and then to Grandmother Jones, and then from Clay to Miss Hattie and finally to Gisele. Without a word, Gisele turns away from Officer Bolin. Miss Hattie hugs Clay to her side, and they look off toward the shoreline.

My gaze strays back to Ray-boy. He looks miserable, waiting for me to turn him in.

Grandmother Jones pats my shoulder.

"Sorry, sir," I say. "I don't really remember what happened."

Ray-boy's mouth drops open. He looks straight at me

then, and I know he's really seeing me, just like he really saw Gisele after he shot her father. Some things do get through to him, after all.

"Did it themselves," shouts Leroy Frye. "I told you! They shot their own."

Ray-boy's mouth works, but no sound comes out. He closes his eyes, then hangs his head.

Leroy Frye isn't finished. "You ought to arrest all of them. Jail might teach them a lesson."

"Stop, Daddy," Ray-boy mumbles.

"What?" Leroy Frye shakes his head like he thinks his ears are broken.

"I said stop," Ray-boy repeats.

"Boy—"

Officer Bolin catches Leroy's hand in mid-backswing, but says nothing.

Ray-boy turns to Officer Bolin. "I had a gun, and I made them get in the car at the Richelieu. Miss Jones, she drove off, and I kept them in a house until they tried to get away. That's when I shot him."

"You shot Sardis?" Officer Bolin rubs his hand over his head. In the gray light of the morning after Camille, he looks almost as broken as the town around us.

"Yes, sir."

Officer Bolin frowns. "It was an accident, wasn't it, boy?"

Ray-boy swallows. He wants to answer yes, I can tell. And if he does, I won't say anything. He takes the waterlogged pistol from his pants. "I got this from—"

"Shut your mouth," snarls Leroy, but Ray-boy turns a shoulder to his father. He hands the pistol to Officer Bolin, who takes it with another deep frown.

He looks from Ray-boy to Leroy. "Damn, Frye. This is a mess."

"Ain't my problem," the bigger Frye growls. The little Frye, Ray-boy, gives me a guilty look and walks away, toward a big heap of sand.

Officer Bolin doesn't do anything for a long, long time. I wonder if he'll arrest Ray-boy, or Ray-boy's daddy, but I figure he probably won't. For a minute, I fear he'll change his mind and arrest us.

What he does is more and more of nothing, except stare at Leroy Frye, who stares back as hateful as ever.

Finally, Officer Bolin dons his hat and glances at us. "Shelter's inland, thirty miles or so. If y'all go to an aid station, they'll transport you."

"Even though we're black?" Grandmother Jones asks.

Officer Bolin frowns, and I see a touch of red creep into his cheeks. "Yes, Mai—er—Mrs.—um, yeah," he finally manages, then clears his throat. "Yes, ma'am."

Leaving him behind, we soon find an aid station and catch a bus. Mixed. Integrated. And everyone seems too tired or beaten to care. Sand stands on the bus floor, several inches deep. The inside smells like the beach at low tide, sour and half dead.

On the way to the Red Cross tent, we pass a pile of concrete blocks where the Richelieu should have been.

"Lord," whispers Grandmother Jones, surveying the wreck.

"I heard people talking about that. Those folks, they all died," says an old white woman with wet gray hair hanging to her shoulders. "All the people who stayed, save for one girl who floated out her window and held on to couch cushions and a tree. The wind and the water nearly beat her to death."

When the bus stops, the old woman seems confused. Disoriented.

"Come with us," Miss Hattie says, and she takes the woman's hand.

We climb over stones and boards to a tent, where we huddle until another bus carries us to a white school north of the coast. Even this place is coated with sand, but at least it smells bleached and clean. When the wind blows, more sand spits and trickles through any crack. Even the tiniest opening.

Hours pass in the shelter. I've gotten dry clothes now, a brown dress, not sewed well like Grandmother Jones can do.

My throat feels near parched, because the water from the tap runs red and black and brown. Some of it stinks like sewage. Grandmother Jones tells me not to drink, says it's all contaminated. The shelter workers tell us they'll bring us fresh water as soon as they can find some. And food, and medicine for people with cuts and sickness.

News of the storm filters in across that day and the next.

"Gulfport and Biloxi are gone," says one man.

"Over five hundred miles of road impassable," says another.

"One hundred thousand tons of debris," announces radio news.

When we have power and when it works, the television shows pictures of barges and navy ships thrown miles inland, and destruction from tornados and floods all the way to Tennessee, and threats of more floods across the Blue Ridge Mountains, all the way to the East Coast. Hundreds are thought dead or feared dead, maybe as many as two hundred and fifty, plus three in Cuba.

I record these things in my journal, on pages now brittle after drying out, and I write to myself instead of Ba.

I'm sure she won't mind.

It feels good to look at what is, what might be, instead of always at what was.

"Pass Christian is just about gone except for the old Maritime Academy," Miss Hattie tells us over a bread and bacon dinner half an hour after Crazy Sardine arrives. His leg is stitched from a flesh wound where the bullet grazed him, and he seems very happy Ray-boy was a rotten shot.

"They say the wind was over two hundred miles an hour," he says. "And they got sand pushed miles up Highway 90 from that thirty-five-foot storm surge."

"That witch was evil," says Gisele.

Crazy Sardine laughs at her. "What are you talking about, child? Camille was a hurricane, not a witch."

The adults go on talking.

Gisele and Clay stare at me, and I shrug.

"Why don't they remember?" Clay asks, almost under his breath.

"People see what they need to see," I tell him. "It's up to us to remember the truth and do right by it."

Gisele raises her hand and twists it, and sings some words from my storm chant. A little breeze blows across the top of my water, and I shake a finger at her. "Not inside. Never conjure wind inside, unless it's an emergency."

Clay laughs into his hand.

"What we going to do, Maizie?" asks Miss Hattie, breaking bacon onto her bread.

Grandmother Jones sighs. "Go home when we can, I suppose. Rebuild, like everyone else."

"Zashar gonna come back?" Gisele asks where only I can hear her.

"No," I say. "She's gone for good, I think. But we'll do what we can to help tame the winds when they blow again. We'll always have storms to fight."

"I'll be ready if my turn comes," she swears, and she opens her palm. Etched on her hand in crude ink I see a blue lump with teeth. An Amazon crocodile.

I smile at her and make a crocodile mouth with my fingers, and I snap the jaws shut.

She grins.

"Y'all stop that alligator nonsense," says Grandmother Jones. She doesn't quote Dr. King or anyone else, and her smile comes quickly.

*"Oui, Grand-mère,"* I answer, and she kisses the top of my head without even correcting my French.

# HISTORICAL NOTES

**Hurricane Camille.** Hurricane Camille was the first Category 5 storm to hit the United States in modern times. As depicted in the story, Hurricane Camille hit the Gulf Coast late on Sunday, August 17, 1969. Wind gusts reached more than two hundred miles per hour. The "storm surge," or waters pushed in by the tropical depression and fierce winds, reached twenty and thirty feet, obliterating whatever the winds failed to destroy. Huge boats were tossed inland like toys. Pieces of straw were driven through trees like arrows. Houses, businesses, hotels, docks, and bridges were erased as if they had never existed. An estimated five hundred miles of roads were blocked by more than one hundred thousand pounds of debris. Pass Christian, Mississippi, saw the highest water levels, over thirty-five feet in some places. Cleanup from this storm took months, and even today, the scars of Camille can be seen along Mississippi's Gulf Coast.

**The Kingdom of Dahomey, the "Real" Amazons, and African-African Slavery.** Africa's Kingdom of Dahomey was, arguably, one of the first societies in modern times ever to grant status to women. All men in power were required to have a *kpojito*, a female "double" to advise them on every decision made. Women could inherit property, serve as head of household, and occupy cherished positions such as bodyguards to kings centuries before women obtained such rights in American society.

For all the legends about fierce women in battle, only the war women of Dahomey have verified basis in historical fact. As early as the 1700s, European visitors to this complex African nation called them *Amazons*. Reports of the Amazons continued until 1892, when better-armed French Legionnaires defeated the forces of King Behanzin.

Dahomey's Amazons lived in palatial fortresses as large as four miles square. Girls entered service in childhood, severing ties with their birth families. Even children of slaves were eligible if they demonstrated strength and courage enough to impress the older Amazons. Amazons were considered wives of the king, and would fight to the last woman to defend him.

The Amazons were Dahomey's "front line" army, and the sight of them often terrified enemies into retreat. They did shave their heads, file their teeth, and soak and shape their fingernails into near daggers to increase their fearsome appearance. Preferred weapons were clubs, machetes, and muskets. Only the youngest Amazons used the bow and arrow, and arrows were usually tipped with poison.

Most legends and stories concerning the Amazons, their dress, and their customs related in this story are as accurate as possible, based on available historical documents; however, it was sometimes difficult because of the racist and ethnocentric ("my culture is better than your culture") views of the Europeans who recorded Amazon feats.

King Agaja indeed closed Dahomey's slave trade for a time, and some believe he did this in protest of the practice. Others believe he did this to gain control of the market. Almost all identified West African societies participated in the practice of enslaving each other, and in selling black slaves to New World traders. Before the interference of white society, however, this practice proceeded between tribes much as it did between Native American tribes in the United States. Slaves were captured as "spoils of war," and many were brought into the tribal folds and made "family," eventually living as full, equal, and productive members of that tribe. Slaves were often used for exchange, barter, and even treaty making.

With white traders came the profit motive for slavery,

and more important, guns. Better weapons made for better warfare, and African leaders soon engaged in a deadly struggle to arm themselves against increasingly dangerous neighbors. Tribal customs were rapidly destroyed. By the mid-1800s, slavery in many West African nations was as brutal, oppressive, and deadly as it was in the United States.

Would African-African slavery have come to this had whites not interfered? Would Africans have resolved their internal conflicts and slave practices on their own? These are questions that can't be answered, but they remain the subject of healthy debate.

**The "Climate" of 1969 and Today**. Freedom Summer in 1964 was a multigroup, multicultural effort to break through racial barriers in one of America's most closed societies: the state of Mississippi. Their misson was registering people to vote. Hundreds of volunteers trained for weeks before arriving. Training topics included how to protect themselves during a beating, how to handle themselves if arrested, and how to operate in chains and pairs to avoid being separated and killed. And even with such training, volunteers died. Volunteers were beaten, maimed, and harassed. Both local and non-local workers risked life and limb every day to fight for changes they believed were right and moral.

## Historical Sources

Alpern, S. B. (1999). *Amazons of Black Sparta: The Women Warriors of Dahomey.* New York: New York University Press.

Bay, E. G. (1998). *Wives of the Leopard: Gender, Politics, and Culture in the Kingdom of Dahomey.* Richmond: University Press of Virginia.

Edgerton, R. B. (2000). *Warrior Women: The Amazons of Dahomey and the Nature of War.* University of California (Los Angeles): Westview Press.

Erenrich, S. and the Cultural Center for Social Change (1999). *Freedom Is a Constant Struggle: An Anthology of the Mississippi Civil Rights Movement.* Montgomery, AL: Blackbelt Press.

Payne, C. M. (1995). *I've Got the Light of Freedom: The Organizing Tradition and the Mississippi Freedom Struggle.* University of California (Los Angeles): University of California Press.

University of Southern Mississippi Libraries (2000). USM McCain Library and Archives: Civil Rights in Mississippi Digital Archive.

Weather Channel Enterprises, Inc. (1995–2000). *Storms of the Century: Hurricane Camille* Part I–Part IV.